MAFIA'S FAKE BRIDE

MAFIA'S OBSESSION
BOOK TWO

SUMMER COOPER

LOVY BOOKS

Matteo stared out at the darkness beyond the mansion windows, lost in thought. He'd finally arrived in the small Louisiana town to discover a veritable mansion waited for him. He'd been in that Lamborghini 400 GT for two days, and his body refused to get into it again. Too bad for his body that he took orders from someone that didn't give two fucks what his body wanted.

A glass of scotch sat on the windowsill, forgotten until he reached for it. The ice had melted, but it didn't matter. He needed the alcohol to soothe his mind, to help him get to sleep. The pain in his back would stop eventually and he'd be able to relax. He'd had a lot of time to think on the way down here and he knew he had a lot to get done.

Tomorrow would be soon enough, he decided. He'd had a meal, a shower, and now he was in his library, staring out at the foreign darkness beyond. He could see nothing but trees beyond the manicured grass at the side of the huge house. Beyond that, he knew there would probably be swamps filled with mosquitos and alligators.

He was down here for two reasons, the file told him. To collect a debt from a woman no doubt beaten down by time and to branch out his organization's empire. The second part he'd start later in the week when he met with a man named Jeffrey. The other part he had to start tomorrow. He didn't like it, but he had to do it.

His fingers tightened on the small glass until it shattered in his hand. Matteo quickly stood up, cleared the shattered shards from his pants, and tossed them in a trashcan. The glass had been drained at some point, even though he'd forgotten about it once again. He filled another glass and walked up to his bedroom.

Once he'd changed and settled into his bed, his mind began to race again. Back to a few days ago, when he'd been summoned by his aunt to her palace of a home in New York. Three brownstone apartments had been torn apart inside to create a huge amount of space that most people in New York would give their eyeteeth for. The outside façade hadn't been changed, it still looked as though there were three apartments from the outside, but there wasn't. The Alfonsi Mafia had money, they just didn't want to scream it out to the world.

Because part of being in the Mafia was keeping that membership a secret. You didn't shout about it to the rooftops as Andy Rossi did, the little shit. It was his fault Matteo had to leave New York to get the police off his back. He was the reason Celeste Alfonsi, Matteo's maternal aunt, called him to her palace in the first place.

The current head of the Alfonsi crime-syndicate got her position by marriage. She was married to Nick Alfonsi when he was taken out by a rival group. A group that had since been wiped off the face of the map, thanks to Celeste. The tall, statuesque woman with the strikingly cold brown eyes was ruthless, far more ruthless than Nick had ever been, Matteo had been told.

Nick hadn't really wanted the role he'd been given by birth; he'd only wanted the money it brought to him. He'd used it to pay for whores, gambling, and drinking. Wasted it, according to Celeste. She wouldn't have anymore waste. She'd brought the syndicate out of drug peddling and into gambling and guns. The cops didn't sniff around so much when it came to gambling and guns, at least until Andy started to run his mouth.

That's when Celeste called in her sister's son because now the police were looking at him too. They had to get the heat off of him, and she had a plan. A plan that Matteo knew would cost him something, if not physically, at least mentally. His aunt was one bloodthirsty bitch, even if she deserved some of that blood she so craved.

He was the only son for either the Mazza or the Alfonsi line so when it came time to choose an heir, Celeste chose him. Celeste wanted a man to take over her business when she was ready to give up the reins. She'd taken over raising her sister Angelica's son. She'd supervised his upbringing since he was seven years old and had raised him as the son her husband, Nick, hadn't given her before his death. She'd never been a mother to Matteo, she'd been a taskmaster to be feared, and Matteo had given her the respect she demanded.

He didn't like her, but she didn't care about that. She wanted an heir, a prince who would be king to her mighty throne. Even if she wasn't known as a queen.

His thoughts drifted further into that day, sitting in her study, lined in dark woods and books she'd probably never read. Matteo doubted anyone had ever cracked the spines of those books, if they were real books. For all he knew, there were no words written in those pages, only blank paper made to fill out the ornate leather spines of the ornaments.

"I need you to go to Louisiana," she'd started her audience with a command. For that's what it was, a command, not a request.

"Alright. What am I to do down there?" He'd sat on the small pink leather-covered loveseat, made for tiny people in a bygone era, certainly not for a man of his size.

"I need you to collect a long-owed debt, Matteo, one that has been a long time coming." Her hard brown eyes had drilled into his.

Brown eyes were usually described as soft, warm, mellow, honeyed even, but never hard. Hers couldn't be described as anything but hard. There was a note of something even harder than amber in her brown eyes. Maybe petrified wood would be more appropriate.

He tapped at the glass of scotch in his hand, a glass of scotch he didn't sip at all while he was with her. It was there for show, after all. He knew better than to drink anything she'd poured, not because it might be poisoned, though it might be. No, he didn't drink in front of her because mere mortals were not allowed to take any kind of sustenance in her presence, even if she'd offered it, except at the dinner table. So, he held the glass and waited.

He had an inkling of why he was being sent to Louisiana, the cops were heavy after Andy Rossi, the loud-mouthed prick. He couldn't keep anything to himself, which is why he hadn't wanted to take the man into his organization, but his aunt had over-ridden his worries because he was the son of an old friend of hers. Fat lot of good that had done them.

"I assume you've made all the arrangements?" he asked in a monotone voice, it wouldn't do to sound like he didn't want to go or doubted her abilities. Even now, at 32, he gave her the respect she'd beaten out of him as a child. It was a hard habit to break, even as a grown man. She could order him dead, or poison him at dinner if she chose to.

He watched as she tapped at her glass with scarlet painted fingernails shaped into dagger-like points. The nails were too long to be useful, merely for show then, and a sign that she was a woman who performed no manual labor. And dangerous, just like her. His eyes narrowed on her as she spoke again.

"I'm thinking of retiring after you complete this task. It's time for me to explore Italy a little more, enjoy the fruits of my labors. And it's time for you to earn your living." She'd looked away from him, her iron-gray hair a mass of waves down her back. She wore a black shirt by some Italian designer paired with black slacks. They both showed off a frame kept slim not from exercise but from the nervous energy she could not get rid of.

"I see." He paused, trying to think of a sentence that might be appropriate but not judgmental, that she could twist to her ways. "I will do as you wish."

It was the most noncommittal thing he could think of to say. You had to think carefully around Celeste, choose your words wisely. "I will do my best" might mean you'd done shoddy work before but wouldn't now. "I will settle this matter quickly" could mean you wanted the old bat gone and out of your hair, which would be such a no-no with her. You had to step carefully with her, otherwise, you might lose your head.

"Good. I've arranged a house for you, a car, and help while you are there. The details are in this file, along with the keys to the house and the car. It's a long drive, but I want that car to be seen around town."

He didn't ask her why she wanted the car seen, or how long he should be gone. He knew there'd be a timeline in there some-where. Celeste would have taken care of even the minutest detail within that timeline and if he deviated, there'd be hell to pay.

He controlled his urge to inhale deeply and stood to take the file from her. He held his hand out and she slid the file across her desk.

"I'll have Andy taken care of while you're down in Louisiana, so make sure people notice you when you're there. Go out every day, interact in the community, but not too much." She paused to pin him to the floor with her eyes. "Don't bring the cops on you down there."

"Yes, Aunt." He inclined his head, mainly so he wouldn't have to look at her lined face or the bright-red lipstick she still insisted on wearing. He repeated the mantra from his youth, the one that always kept him in check. "Just obey, just obey, just obey." That was all he had to do. Just obey.

"There was debt that your uncle was owed before he died. One that he wasn't able to collect because, well, he died." She

rolled her eyes like it was the long-dead Nick's fault for dying. "I want that debt collected before I go anywhere. She's owed it to me for almost 27 years now. It's time she paid up."

This was some debt then. Matteo suspected he knew who it was, he'd heard whispers over the years, and had once spent an evening reading old newspaper articles and wiki pages about his uncle's death. He'd died with a movie starlet in his car, a movie starlet that was pregnant at the time. She'd disappeared into obscurity, never to be heard from again, but Matteo knew that Celeste hadn't forgotten.

She'd been humiliated over the circumstances of Nick's death, that he'd been out all night with the starlet and then had the gall to die in the car she was in. He couldn't even live long enough to die alone in the ambulance or the hospital. Oh no, he'd died with that starlet's arms around him. Not that Celeste would have been anywhere near Nick's no doubt bloodied body, Matteo had mused. She wouldn't defile herself like that.

And now she'd decided it was time for payback. Matteo took the manila folder and left the study without another word. There didn't need to be, Celeste would take anything he had to say now as questioning, and Celeste was not to be questioned. If he had a question, he had to find the answer himself.

He drove back home in his dark blue Maserati Ghibli S G4 GranSport, a gift from his aunt when he graduated from NYU with a business degree. An old car now but he still loved and maintained it to the highest standards, his own. He thought as he drove carefully, skillfully, along the congested roads that would take him back to his apartment on the outskirts of the city.

He glanced at the file when he stopped for a red light but didn't pick it up. He would wait and think for now. She'd taught him that, to think carefully before he took action. He'd have to put quite a few things on hold here to take care of business down there, but it didn't matter. There'd be someone to deal with those matters, his aunt would make sure of it.

He pulled into the parking garage of his building and parked on the top floor. This was the floor that held the elevator for his part of the building, the very top. He used a keycard to get into the elevator and then into the sole penthouse apartment. His view allowed him to see the tallest buildings in the city that he liked to look at but didn't necessarily like to be in. His keys went on the hook beside the door and his shoes, loafers of the finest Italian leather, came off and went into a small nearby closet.

The press of a button turned on the sound system and Sting began to croon about fields and desert beauties. He went into his dark living room, turned on a lamp made from some kind of salt the designer told him about, and sat on the leather sectional sofa. With his back against the couch arm, he opened the file and began to read.

The first few pages were old magazine pages, interviews the starlet, Ruby Heinz, had given a very long time ago. They were typical of the era and talked about the furnishings in the room and the clothing brands she wore. She told the interviewer about her movie project and how she'd had to reach deep to portray her character accurately, to identify with the woman she'd played.

The article didn't mention that the apartment and clothes had been paid for by Celeste's husband, or that she was pregnant at the time. Those were matters that were noted by more pages. Lease payment records, store receipts, and the hospital records and payment receipts for one Ruby Hebert, AKA Ruby Heinz.

There was no further background information. It would seem the woman had come from the swamps and had left a trail of secrecy behind her. People wouldn't talk down there and that had frustrated Celeste, no doubt.

There was no mention of what had happened to her child or where she'd worked since the day she left New York and the movies behind. Just an address, written in cursive, on a piece of cheap notebook paper. Interesting.

Matteo got up to make himself a scotch he could drink and went back over the file one more time.

That had been four days ago. Now he was in a house hermetically sealed to protect those inside from the sultry heat of a Louisiana summer night, trying to figure out what to do next. He wanted to run away, forget he had this job, forget who his aunt was, who *he* was, but years of training wouldn't let him quit or run away. He was meant to be a Mafia king, and that was all he knew how to be. So, that's what he'd do.

1

Two Days Later

Matteo learned a lot in the two days since he'd arrived in Louisiana. The first thing he learned was a young woman was living with the target. Ruby Hebert, according to the report he'd found online, had lived at the same address with the same girl since she'd left New York.

He'd paid for the report from an online data-broker. It turned out the girl, now a woman, was Ruby's daughter, Marie. There'd been a school picture for the young woman, and an old picture from the DMV for Ruby. The young girl was cute, in the way young girls were, but she was of no interest to Matteo. Too young and not part of the job. His target was Ruby.

Further digging showed that Ruby was now an invalid and taken care of by her daughter. Which meant he'd have to take an interest in the daughter. This bit of news changed things and he'd had to email Celeste about it.

She'd come up with a new plan, a plan that involved him wooing the daughter. Whether she was attached to someone or not. The way she saw it, some backwater bumpkin from the sticks would be happy to leave any kids and a husband behind for a man like Matteo. Then, he'd dump her, with her life in shambles and with her mother's debt to pay, due on demand.

He'd almost run away at that point when he'd read the email. Most people would say fine, you can't get blood out of a turnip, but not Celeste. She wanted Ruby to pay, and if that meant using the daughter to do it, then so be it. If it got him that one step closer to his goal, he'd do it.

He wouldn't like himself, but Matteo knew he hadn't liked himself very much since Celeste took over his upbringing. She'd turned a bright, intelligent, happy young boy into a somber, watchful robot that barely felt... anything. His father had disappeared a long time ago before he was even born, but his mother was still alive.

Matteo couldn't even respond emotionally to her, which was why he hadn't seen her in months now; maybe it had even been a year, he wasn't sure and didn't care. Emotions were not something he allowed himself to feel. Especially when Celeste was near him. He just shut down completely when he was near her.

Being this far away felt good, really good, but he knew she was there, in the back of his mind. She would be waiting, judging, ready to use anything, and anyone, for her brutal version of revenge. Not that she didn't deserve some kind of revenge, her husband had been a cheater, and then he'd died because of his activities. With his lover, not his wife.

Nick, Celeste's now dead husband, had branched out their organization, had started to creep into territory that wasn't his, and it cost him his life. Of course, those activities had allowed Celeste the life she loved, but Matteo wouldn't point that out. He inhaled slowly, deeply, and then walked away from the laptop.

The sound of a bell told him he had a new notification and he walked back over to the laptop. He didn't want to look at the new email, but it might be important. A click of the mouse opened up a new screen and he saw a picture of a very timid looking young woman. It was her driver's license photo and she stared straight into the camera, no smile, no emotion at all. Just a dead gaze that still managed to stir… *something* in him.

A frown marred his features as he increased the size of the photo. So, this was Marie now. Well, from her latest license, at least. He stared at the image for a moment before he closed the picture and read the text within the email. It seemed Marie's mother no longer drove, but Marie did drive her mother's car out every day, around one in the afternoon, to do the shopping and other errands.

He wrote back to the data broker to tell them it was good work and then glanced at the clock. It was about the time the young woman drove into town, so he picked up the keys to the old car that his aunt had provided.

The 1966 Lamborghini 400 GT was the very same one his uncle had died in. Celeste paid to have the damned thing restored for some reason, and now he was expected to drive it around town. Matteo assumed it was to creep Marie's mother out, to frighten her, but the woman never left her bed, so the whole thing was pointless. It drove smoothly and had a few updates to make it suitable in the modern world, so he didn't mind too much.

With a cold gaze hidden behind mirrored aviator sunglasses, he drove into the small town, careful to keep his speed down. He wasn't in a rush because he was waiting to spot the girl. He figured she'd stop off at the grocery store first. With a twist of his wrist, the car turned smoothly into a gas station where he filled up the almost full tank. He glanced around and saw her, over in the parking lot across the street.

He didn't know for sure, but he was almost certain she was staring right at him. He felt his lips twitch in satisfaction, his target had been located. He put a debit card into the machine, paid for his fuel, and then slowly drove across the road and into the parking lot of the grocery store.

Matteo noted she was distracted as she put the groceries away. She turned to return the empty cart to the stand, then stopped, obviously lost in thought. He drove on but slammed on the brakes suddenly so that it made a noise. He felt a prickle of guilt, not enough to make him feel sorry, but he felt it.

She responded with a turn, fear clear on her face as she stumbled a little. Her hands were on the hood as he stepped out of the car, all that was good and humble as he apologized to her.

He wasn't aware of what he said, or what she said. All

he could do was note how white and perfect her teeth were, how beautiful and haunting her eyes were, and just how long those tanned legs of hers were in those tiny denim shorts she had on. The t-shirt tented over full breasts that drew his gaze for only a heartbeat, it was those eyes that fascinated him.

His thoughts flew right out of his head for a moment as he looked at her and took in just how odd he felt when he saw her up close. The pictures had done her no justice at all because she had a lovely, heart-shaped face, clear tanned skin, and the cutest button of a nose.

Matteo wasn't completely dead inside, he still liked to have a woman when the mood struck. Usually, they were women that knew the score and were in it for what they could get out of him. This woman was all innocence and charm. There was no kind of guile in her eyes, no knowing twist to her full, luscious lips. And all of that black hair of hers made his hands itch in ways to touch her that he'd never felt before.

He came back to reality briefly, gave her his card, and apologized once more. The target had been acquired and the first contact had been made. That was all he needed to do for now. He left her to carry on with her errands and went into the store to buy a few things, so nobody would notice that he'd gone into the parking lot but not gone into the store.

His aunt wanted him to be noticed so he went over to the library briefly, picked out a book, and got himself a library card. He left there and drove on, thoughts of the girl, the woman rather, still on his mind. He turned on a playlist he kept hidden in his phone and hit play. The sound of The Beatles filled the car as he drove back to the mansion hidden down a bayou path.

It wasn't until he was in the driveway, the voice of John Lennon in his head, that he realized he felt something he hadn't felt in a long time. Desire tinged with something he thought might be hope. That made him blink a few times before he turned the car off and stepped out.

Now, why would a girl from the back of beyond in Louisiana make him *feel* anything? Was that what had happened to his late Uncle Nick? He'd met a woman that he couldn't take his eyes off of, or had she just been another conquest? Matteo was familiar with conquests, women he'd bedded for prestige, women he'd bedded that had refused him, but he'd charmed them over time. They'd given in to him, just for him to dump them after their conquest.

Would this woman be the same? Would he be able to seduce her, as his aunt wanted him to do, and then leave her with a broken heart and a debt she couldn't possibly repay? He'd had another notification about their finances: they were one unexpected bill away from the poorhouse, so he knew the women wouldn't be able to repay his aunt. Would the girl's broken heart be enough for her?

Somehow, Matteo doubted it. The whole situation was far thornier than he'd expected it would be. But then, he'd expected a woman like any other, easily conquered and discarded. Something about this young woman told him that wasn't going to be the case.

He thought he'd be able to keep his heart out of it, he

had little doubt about that, but would he be able to forget her? That was a question he didn't want to examine too closely, so he went out to the pool instead. A few laps would keep him focused, and when he went to rest an hour later, his mind was clear.

He had a mission; he would do his duty.

He owed his allegiance to Celeste and the family. Make that family with a capital F. That's who would protect him, serve him, make him their king. This girl meant nothing to him, and he'd do what was expected of him.

She stayed on his mind throughout the night, however, and when he went to bed, it was her he dreamed of. Long, slow kisses made him hum with pleasure, even in his sleep, as he stroked the full breasts, he'd barely noted earlier that day. She wrapped herself around him, eager to know his touch.

At that moment, in that place, Matteo finally felt free of the mental restraints that had shackled his thoughts for so long and he surged against Marie's body with his own. He was just as eager as she was; he craved the devotion those dark brown eyes of hers promised him; craved the solace of her embrace. Even more than that, he accepted it all from her, he expected it, demanded it as the moments passed and he felt her soft body melt into his.

Every inch of her was cradled against him and he slipped the shoulder of the white gown off her shoulders, to kiss the smooth skin there. He inhaled deeply, about to lose control, but he restrained himself, just for now, just until she begged him for more, for all of him.

The gown slipped lower, to the very tops of her breasts,

and Matteo shuddered as he let his lips skim the plump flesh. She felt so good, so right. Nothing, no one, had ever felt so right in his entire life, and he felt the pulse of that sensation deep inside his abdomen as a twist of pleasure. It was a pleasure that radiated out, to the very part of him that he wanted to bury inside of her.

"Marie, you're mine. You'll always be mine," he murmured against the tops of her breasts as he felt her shuddering response against his own body. It only made him hungrier for her.

His hands moved from her waist to her back, to lift her against the wall so that he could cradle himself between her heated thighs. It was so warm there, so promisingly wet, that he could feel her against his suddenly naked body. He didn't know how his clothes disappeared or why, and didn't care, he just wanted to move, to pull back far enough to bury himself inside what he instinctively knew was her virgin sheath.

He'd pulled back, teeth set, ready to hold back as she took him inside of her body for the very first time. A piercing sound infiltrated the moment, destroyed it, as reality invaded. He was dreaming, that noise was his phone. Fuck.

He rolled over to answer the ring and saw it was Celeste. He couldn't quite shut down as he normally did when he had to speak to her, but he faked it well.

"Yes, Aunty?" he asked in a bland voice, no sign of his anger at her or tiredness to be found in his voice at all.

"Did you meet the girl yet, Matteo?" Celeste came

straight to the point, without even the courtesy of saying hello.

"I have, Aunty. She's going to be… pliable, I believe," he reported, despite the inner voice in his head telling him to hang up and get back to fucking the sweet temptation that had filled his dream. Would he be able to recapture that moment now?

"Good. You need to do this carefully, Matteo. By that I mean don't invite her to dinner tomorrow and fuck her tomorrow night." Celeste had always been able to cut to the heart of the matter, and when the moment called for crudity, she could use it. Even if it was her nephew she spoke to. "I want her well and truly in love with you by the time you have your way with her. Then, you're going to crush her, do you understand me, Matteo? No gentle letting down, no sweet parting, I want her crushed."

"Yes, Aunty," he said without a hint of emotion.

"Good. And Matteo? Don't fall in love with the little guttersnipe, do you hear me? It wouldn't do at all." Celeste was just as cruel to him as she was to anyone else. He heard the sound of her nails tapping against the wood of her desk and cringed. He hated her, but she was the head of the family.

He would do as instructed.

2

Present Day

You'd think the vultures would wait at least a month before they started to circle, Marie thought a week after her mother's funeral. She stared down at a pile of bills, a pile that she knew she could not pay. Final demands for payment, notices of new bills to be paid, and a warning from several that if Marie didn't find a way to pay the bills, they'd take her to court and take the house from her.

They should have switched the house into Marie's name a long time ago, she realized. But even that wouldn't save her, she thought as she looked around the outdated kitchen. Sunflowers and ducks, that's what her mother had decorated the place with. It had been Marie's refuge for a long time, but now, she could see it with the eyes of a buyer. Outdated, and in desperate need of money that Marie didn't have.

She'd have to sell the house she decided as she opened another bill, this one from a doctor she didn't even remember seeing at the hospital. She frowned as she looked at the itemized bill. Smoking cessation therapy? Her mother didn't smoke, why would they charge her for that?

Marie pushed her index finger into the spot between her eyes that ached so much her stomach started to turn. Some of these charges should be against the law, but she knew there was little she could do about them. Her fingers moved from her forehead down to the space between her mouth and her nose.

What the hell was she going to do?

The last couple of weeks had been hard. First, her mother had taken a turn for the worse, then she died. The funeral took place in the rain: a sad, lonely send-off for a woman hated by most in the town. Matteo's strange words followed, and then the awkward hell of trying to get used to being in the house on her own. She'd barely slept those first few nights, but now it wasn't as bad.

Marie grieved for the first few days, but it was more grief for what should have been and now never would be. She'd grieved for a long time, she knew, even before her mother passed away. The woman had been hard, unlovable, and cruel. Still, she was Marie's mother, but it was time to get on with life.

Now, she was faced with an ever-growing stack of bills and the reality that she'd have to leave her home. The only home she'd ever known, she thought as she got up from the table to go into the living room. She'd sell what she could, get rid of the house, and maybe she'd go somewhere new.

Everyone in this town treated Marie as if she was tainted because of her mother. She had no real friends here, nobody that would miss her. She sat on the couch and let her gaze drift into space. She could go to New Orleans, get a job as a PCA there, and live a carefree life in a town that rarely slept. Or she could go to New York if Matteo ever went back there.

If he wanted her to go back there with him, that is. He might want to end it with her, even if she'd started to wonder if he loved her. There'd been a few hints that he might, and she knew she cared about him deeply. Maybe there was something there, but then again, maybe she only wanted to see what she wanted to see.

He'd been so distant at her mother's funeral, and he hadn't contacted her since then. She knew he'd had to go to New York, but he hadn't even texted her to check on her. He might have been done with her and ready to move on now that he'd had her. That made her blood turn cold, despite the heat of the day. He wouldn't be that cruel, would he?

She knew he could be hard, just as hard as her mother, but did he have that same cruel streak that she had? Marie didn't think so. She wanted to trust him despite those strange words he'd said to her. What did he have to tell her about her mother?

Anxiety began to eat at her, and her stomachache became a tightness that nearly took her breath away. She calmed herself by listing the places she could go to now that she was free. Because, over the passing days, without the daily routine of caring for her mother, without every thought being tied to her mother in some way, Marie came to see that she was free. It had taken a very long time, but at last, she was free of her mother's hatred, her bile, and her stranglehold.

The foot that held her down by the neck to the floor was gone, and she could get up, dust herself off, and see the world if she wanted to. Well, if she could afford to, that is. She felt her lips twitch into a smile as she thought about the places she could go. Las Vegas, Los Angeles, to the palm trees and beautiful beaches of Hawaii maybe? Or Alaska, up to the cold mountains, glaciers, and icy streams that would freeze away her cares.

The world was her home now, and she just had to decide where to head first. Once she sold all the stuff in the house, and the house, and maybe even the car. No, she'd need the car, she'd have to hang onto that somehow.

Her phone buzzed against the back of her thigh and she dug it out to look at the screen. Her heart thudded back into overdrive the minute she saw his name. At last, he'd sent her a text.

"I'll see you tonight, at 8 pm, for dinner. See you soon." Matteo had typed to her.

She felt fear seize at the galloping muscles of her heart as she read it over and over. She couldn't exactly explain why she felt so afraid of the few words he'd sent, but something about the whole situation had set off alarm bells and they wouldn't stop.

With a tired sigh, she got up from the couch and headed

for the bathroom. She needed to get ready, and that meant taking care of things she'd neglected for over a week. A nice hot bath to start her off would be great, she decided and opened the taps to let the water fill the tub.

She wondered what the house would be worth, a distraction for herself, as she stared at the tub. Someone would either have to love the tacky style that ruled in the 1990s to buy the house or have a lot of money to update the entire place. It could be done; the foundations were solid, the walls and roof good, it was just the décor and the floor coverings that would need to be replaced.

She decided she'd find a realtor as she sank into the heated water and felt her muscles respond immediately. They'd know what they were doing and would go after the best price they could get. They worked on commission, she thought but wasn't sure. It didn't matter, as long as it was enough to pay off the bills and leave her with something to live on for a month or two, she'd be fine.

It wasn't like her mother had cared enough to try and leave her an inheritance. Her father hadn't known about her long enough to leave her one either. She'd sometimes wondered as a little girl if there *was* an inheritance for her, sitting forgotten in some lawyer's drawer up in New York, but she had no idea how to find out if there was. Her father had been rich, her mother told her, a tough guy that ruled some kind of gang or something.

Her mother had always warned her to stay away from Mafia guys like there was just a constant parade of men in the Mafia in their town. It was silly, but she'd always warned Marie with hatred in her eye. Stay away…

Well, her mother had taught her a lesson at least. Trust nobody; not your mother, not those in the Mafia, and not the townspeople that had turned their backs on Marie because of her mother. That was something else her mother taught her - don't make a mistake because you will be judged.

Marie sank beneath the water to drive the thoughts out of her mind before she tangled herself into a wreck of angsty hatred of everyone. That wasn't who she was. A quick swipe of her face with a towel and Marie finished the rest of her bath. She didn't want to spend ages soaking when she could be doing something else.

She kept seeing the message he'd sent to her as she dried her hair and dressed. It finally occurred to her what was so *wrong* about it. He'd given her an order, not a request as he normally did. There'd been no question about whether she was busy, whether she was alright, how she was faring, none of that. It was just a "be here and don't give me any other answer" kind of text.

Her brows knitted together as she put on a pair of jeans, followed by a white pullover shirt, and then her shoes. Okay, so he could be a little bossy sometimes. Was she about to start taking orders from him?

If she refused would he drop her? That made an ache start in the center of her chest and she decided she'd brush it off for now. She knew he had a lot on at the moment too, he was a busy guy. He'd probably just written it in haste and hadn't thought about the way it would come across.

With that settled in her mind, she pushed the rest of her worries away. One final thing nagged at her though. He'd said they needed to talk about her mother or something like that. She couldn't remember the exact way he'd put it now. Then he'd told her he was leaving for a few days and that had been the memory that stuck, the fact that he'd walked away. Did a man do that when he knew his woman needed him? She wouldn't know, she had no experience with relationships that went that far.

Too much worry and too much time had passed since that brief conversation for her to remember it exactly. She was at the door and paused to look back at the quiet house. It had never been this quiet, not for a long time, anyway. The only noise was the hum of the refrigerator and that was it. The sound of her mother's oxygen machine was gone, the sound of her air conditioner and the television.

It was almost disturbing, that lack of sound. She'd become accustomed to it and having someone in the house. Now, it was empty, and she was the only one that inhabited the rooms. Maybe the place did need a family, a couple with kids to replace the anger, sadness, and pain that had soaked into the walls, with joy and laughter instead. A melancholy smile passed over her face as she locked the door and walked out to her old car.

The drive over to Matteo's was done in silence. She was too nervous to play anything, afraid to put her mind into a state that would only be devastated if he told her he was finished with her. She'd become used to playing happy, romantic songs on her way to see him, but now she left the music off. It wouldn't do to build her expectations only to find them crushed when she arrived.

He had wanted her there for dinner, she reminded

herself as she braked for a stop sign. Her fingers tapped on the steering wheel, the darkness now almost complete. She switched her headlights on, pulled out after a red sports car passed her by, and drove on.

Dinner might just be pretense or the prelude to her dismissal. Maybe he'd wanted to end it, but was being kind, giving her time to get over her mother's death. Or maybe she was just being stupid and needed to relax, she thought with a deep breath meant to calm her down. She took another and then another as she turned down the road that would lead her to his house.

Maybe he'd just been busy, as she'd thought earlier. Matteo wasn't the most expressive man in the world, sometimes he looked downright cold, but never when he looked at her. Thoughtful and contemplative perhaps, aroused certainly, happy even a time or two, but never cold. That was for everyone else.

Over the last few weeks, she'd felt that they'd created a world of their own, one where only they existed, and nobody else could break into unless they allowed them to. That hint of the danger he exuded would keep anyone unwanted out of their world, she knew that much.

But what if he turned that around on her? No, she reminded herself, he had been so kind to her throughout the end of her mother's illness, and then at the hospital. He'd been there for her, held her when she needed him when her mother's time came and the woman that had given her life slipped away.

Marie tapped her fingers against the steering wheel and pressed a little harder against the gas pedal. This was not going to be over if she didn't actually arrive there. Cautious as always, Marie didn't like to speed, but a few miles over the speed limit wouldn't hurt, would it?

The glimmer of golden eyes in the wide, water-filled ditch at the edge of the road told her there were wild animals in the darkness, but the road was clear, and she pulled into his driveway without a problem. She paused as she pulled past the gates, took a couple of deep breaths to calm herself down, again, before she ran her fingers through her hair.

It was time to face the music, whatever that music was to be. She didn't think, deep down, that Matteo was about to end things with her, but life had never been overly fair to her. It would be just like fate to give her a glimpse of what she could have, of a life she could have never dreamed of having, only to snatch it away. To Marie, fate was like Puck in Shakespeare's play. Always out to fuck people over if it could.

She had a lifetime of experience to prove that. Only, this once in her life, she held onto a breath of hope. She wanted to be optimistic, to feel confident that all was well between her and the man she was all but certain she'd fallen in love with. If only she didn't also feel a need to place her hands behind her back and cross her fingers to ward off bad luck. All she wanted was to lose herself in him, to let go of her grief and worries. If fate would be so kind as to allow her one more moment of that, she'd be really grateful.

3

The crushing weight of anxiety lifted as soon as Matteo opened the door with a smile that she had a feeling was reserved only for her. Normally his grim-faced man employee answered the door, and that guy made Marie nervous. She stuck her hand out tentatively for Matteo to take it, and he pulled her inside with a laugh.

"What's wrong, Marie?" He kissed her cheek softly, an odd look in his eye. It was gone before she could define it, so she just smiled and leaned into his kiss.

"Nothing, I just thought it might be that guy that normally answers the door." She closed the door and then followed him through the house to the dining room. She eyed him up as they walked through the house and wasn't surprised to find that in the black lounge pants and long black t-shirt, Matteo was just as sexy as he was in a suit. "What are we having?"

"Gumbo, potato salad, and French bread from what the

cook told me." He sat down with a smile that was more of a smirk than anything. "She's so bossy."

"Cajun women can be," Marie said with a husky laugh, though she wasn't sure she'd deem it bossy. More like confident and self-assured in their decisions. "It sounds wonderful."

Matteo guided her to a chair before he took one beside her. He'd asked her how she was doing when the cook came in with a trolley. The table was set with white bowls, saucers, and tableware already so all she had to do was set the food down on the table before she went back out again with a wish that they enjoyed their food.

Marie turned to Matteo with a smile as he ladled gumbo into a bowl. "I'm doing alright. It's weird, being at home alone, but it's not as bad as I thought. I was afraid I'd turn into this blubbering mess that couldn't handle being on her own, but it's not been too bad. After that first night, anyway."

Marie looked away as she didn't want him to see the hurt in her eyes. She'd wanted to ask him to stay with her, to come to her so many times, but he'd told her he'd contact her in a few days. She'd had to assume he'd be busy if he said something like that. Normally, she'd have expected him to ask her to come to stay with him, but maybe she'd made too many assumptions lately.

"Good, I've wanted to come and see you, but, well, things are getting a bit complicated for me down here, and I've spent a lot of hours at the uh-" Matteo looked away, his eyes squinted before he turned back, his face clear, "at the office, basically."

She wasn't stupid. She'd started to catch on that he didn't exactly have an office a while ago. He had to be at a lot of places, though, and take care of a lot of things that he never explained. She didn't ask, because at first, she didn't feel like it was any of her business. Now, well, she was almost afraid to ask. She feared his answer, not his reaction.

"I understand," she assured him and turned her attention to her food. It was spiced perfectly, and everything had blended together nicely in the gumbo. The rest of the food was heavenly too, but almost anything would be after a week of eating cans of ravioli she'd found in the cabinet and sandwiches.

She hadn't seen much point in cooking over the last week, she just didn't have the heart to go to the effort. A bowl of microwaved heart-attack-in-a-can here and a sandwich there wouldn't hurt her, anyway. She hoped.

Dinner was quiet after that and she enjoyed the comfort of not being alone, even if the other person wasn't speaking. She'd been quiet all week, she'd wanted to talk to him, to hear his voice, but he was eating so it would be rude to speak.

"Do you want anything for dessert? I think we have a chocolate cake?" He wiped his mouth and put the napkin down in his now-empty bowl. His eyes smiled at her and her heart skipped when she saw contentment in his eyes.

"No, but a walk outside would be nice." She felt a little closed off inside the house, far too insulated, and wanted the wildness of the outdoors, even if it was only a small dose. The mosquitos were still out and about, so they wouldn't be out for long.

He took her hand and they went out to the back to walk for a little while. They reached the pool, and Marie decided to stop there to watch the lights dance in the water.

"It's mesmerizing, isn't it?" he asked her as she stared down into the depths of the pool.

"It is, yes. I know it's all artificial, it's a pool with electric lights, but it's still so beautiful to watch." She didn't want to admit that his was the only fancy in-ground pool she'd ever seen at night.

"It's not as beautiful as you, Marie." He pulled her to him then and she melted into his side with relief. That relief mingled with desire the minute their lips touched, and she moaned against his mouth.

"That's enough of that," he whispered as he pulled away suddenly, his hands on her shoulders to gently push her away. "Want to watch a movie?"

"I'd rather you took me upstairs, Matteo." She'd decided to go with blunt and to the point. She wanted him, he wanted her, they were both adults, what could possibly be the problem. They'd only had that one night, so far, but she wanted a lifetime of nights like that, of those kinds of moments. She pleaded with him with her eyes, put off the talking, let's do the going to bed.

"I need to talk to you first, baby. Let's get in, away from the mosquitos."

She didn't think her heart could sink any lower than it had already, but when he took her hand to help guide her back into the house, she found out it could. He was serious.

She'd thought he was joking. Who wanted to talk when you could have sex? And talk? Dirty talk was nice, she'd learned, and the way he did it?

Even that memory couldn't put a smile on her face as she followed him into the house. He took her into the living room, and she sat down on the couch while he filled two glasses. One with scotch and the other with the ginger ale she'd asked for. He brought the glasses over, set them down on the table in front of them, and then turned to her.

"I need to tell you some things, things I probably should have told you already." He tried to take her hands but her fingers were too numb to close around his.

"You're married, aren't you?" She knew this was all too good to be true. Damnit!

"What? No, we've talked about that already. I'm not married, darling." He tugged at her fingertips, but she could only stare at him, waiting for the hammer of doom that he was about to drop on her.

"It's nothing like that, it's more about the past." He pursed his lips suddenly, and she could see that he was trying to figure out how to proceed.

"What do you mean the past? You mentioned something about my mom at her funeral. What did you mean?" Dots started to connect in her brain, dots from her hometown here in Louisiana to a place far away, in New York. "You're not my cousin, are you?"

She pulled her hands away and brushed at her arms as her skin began to crawl.

"Fuck no!" he said harshly but cringed. "Sorry, no we're not related. Not really."

"Not really?" Marie's left eyebrow arched elegantly over her eye as she narrowed her eyes at him. "Not really? I need more information than that, Matteo."

She didn't berate him any more than that and didn't demand anything more, mainly because she was afraid of the truth. She didn't want to know what he had to say, what he was about to reveal to her. She didn't want to hear it. She got up from the couch, ready to leave but he followed after her, turned her to him, and back her up into the wall.

"Marie, please? Hear me out? This is going to be huge." He paused, swallowed, took a deep breath, and tried to erase the look of shame off of his face, but failed. "My aunt is your father's widow."

"Who?" She tried to pull away from him, but he was pressed into her and she couldn't move, her body refused to even try when he was that close. The smell of his cologne, his natural scent filled her nose, and her head began to spin.

"Come back to the couch?" He pulled away, and she had to wonder if it was because he was as helpless as she was when he was that close to her. She'd noticed the way his nostrils flared and his head tilted closer to her the longer he was pressed into her.

"Fine." She didn't want to, it was the very last fucking thing she wanted to do, but if he was determined to tear her world apart, she might as well let him get it over with. Because she knew, she just knew, that further explanation would only make what he'd already said even worse. He didn't have to say another word, and she already knew that.

"It's a little confusing, but it's like this. My parents let my aunt adopt me when I was seven. She'd lost her husband, your father, to a car accident, and she needed someone to devote her attention to. She chose me, and they agreed. My parents aren't poor, but she had money beyond even their kind of dreams." He paused, swiped a hand over his face, took a sip of his drink, then continued. "So, no, we're not related. It just so happens that your father was married to my aunt when he died. Your mother isn't my aunt, she's just, well, the woman my aunt's husband had an affair with."

She was back to only being able to stare at him. This was his secret? That he was here for… what exactly? "What does she want? Why did she send you here?"

Instinct alone told her that it had to be her father's wife, his aunt, that had sent him down here.

"Well," he paused to wince before he spoke with sad eyes. "How are your finances, Marie?"

"Pardon? You know what they're like. Non-existent, especially now, without my mother's money coming in, or the check I got for taking care of her. What's that got to do with anything? Matteo? Please, just get to the point."

He looked pained as if he didn't want to carry on but something was forcing him to. "Your mother owed Nick $100,000 at the time of his death. She still owes it to his estate. With interest, that's about half a million now."

Cold waves crashed over Marie as she looked at him

and knew the hammer had well and truly fallen. "Your aunt wants it back, I suppose?"

The words came out cold and calm as if she didn't care either way.

"She does. And sent me to collect it. But I didn't know your mother was ill then, or that you'd be so very wonderful, Marie, you have to believe me."

"I have to believe you?" She pulled her top lip in between her teeth, her mind blank, except for one thing. "Is there more?"

He looked at her as if to plead for mercy from her. From her? When he'd just told her this whole thing had been a lie, little more than a ruse to get half a million dollars out of her mother, half a million that she didn't have. Marie didn't have it either. Did this mean his aunt would have her killed?

Fear replaced the coldness and she blinked up at him, terror now the only thing she felt. Her heart thudded in her chest until he spoke again.

"I have a plan. It might not make sense, but in my world it does. It will buy you time, at the very least." He took a deep breath and stared straight into her eyes. "I know you're brave, Marie. You're smart and wonderful, but before you get incredibly pissed off and hurt and all of that flies out the window, I want you to remember one thing. I want to marry you. The debt will be voided if you marry me." He added an "I hope", under his breath, but she caught it.

"You've lied to me," she started. "You came here to make a fool of me, of my mother, you *used* me."

Marie refused to let him see the tears that stung her eyes as hurt and humiliation flooded throughout her body, flushed her skin to an angry red that only made her more self-conscious. "And now, you want me to marry you, Matteo? Are you *insane?*"

"Marie, no, please. Hear me out, darling. I can fix this if you'll just let me. Please. I didn't know you then, I didn't know how much I'd… want you." He'd stumbled over his words but caught himself. She didn't care.

"No. I'm finished with this. My mother warned me that men would only break my heart, and well, she learned from your uncle. So I guess it's only fitting that I learned it from you, right?" She pulled her hands roughly out of his as she pulled away and turned to stalk out of the room.

"Marie, please don't go. I know I can make this right. Just give me a chance." His voice was a plea, but she could hear the doubt in it. That doubt wasn't what made her walk away, though. It was the fact that he'd come here with a plan, and he'd set out on that plan. None of this had been real. None of it.

4

Marie drove home blindly. She stopped at one point, the tears that scalded her eyes and her cheeks made the world a blurry place and it became too dangerous to drive. There was a wide spot, a place where the parish would sometimes leave sand piles for sandbags during storms, just big enough for her to pull off and let the sobs wrack her body.

He'd lied. He'd deceived her. He'd played her for a fool. How could he?

Her mother's voice, unheard for over a week now, played through her mind.

Men only take what they want from you, don't play a fool, Marie. Just stay away from them.

She'd been right. Even if Marie hadn't wanted to admit it, she had to now; Matteo had used her, which was crystal clear. With an unchecked sob, she leaned over to the passenger seat so that passersby wouldn't see her in there, crying her eyes out like some sad loser.

Eventually, with the music off, and the quiet of the insulated car to protect her from any sounds outside, she calmed down enough to dry her face. She dug around in her bag until she found a package of tissues she'd shoved in there before her mother's funeral, and blew her nose. Why did crying always make everything so much worse, she wondered.

You cried because you were hurt, physically or emotionally; the last thing she needed was a headache, clogged sinuses, and the facial pain that came with it. She dried her cheeks and eyes, sat up, and looked around. She hadn't heard any other cars and saw none. He hadn't followed her home, at least.

With her teeth starting to ache, Marie put the car in drive and pulled back onto the road. The lights cut through the darkness and her thoughts changed as she drew closer to her house.

Anger began to creep in. He'd known all along who she was, and he'd played the lovestruck rich guy perfectly. Her mother might have been envious of his performance it had been so good. He'd played the besotted lover while he betrayed her in the worst way she could think of.

She pulled into her driveway, turned the car off, grabbed her bag, and stomped into the house, her head down to make sure she didn't trip over anything in the darkness. He wanted to marry her, to clear this debt her mother owed to Matteo's aunt? How crazy it all sounded, but he didn't seem to notice that.

With a cry of surprise, she stumbled when her foot skidded. She fell to the floor with a loud bang, her right knee slamming into the ground hard. Her bag flew out of her hands and the contents scattered. Defeat overwhelmed her and she began to cry again, sprawled on the floor with no hope left in her heart.

Her mother had died, she had to sell the house she grew up in because she was broke, and now the man that she was certain she'd fallen in love with was some kind of imposter. Or something like that.

She rolled over to her back, thought about getting up for some ice to put on her knee, and dismissed the idea. She just… didn't care.

In her former life, before Matteo, she took as good care of herself as she could. She was the only one that would always be there for her mother. She had to be healthy. Now, it didn't really matter. To anyone.

Even Matteo wanted to use her for his own ends. She wasn't sure why he wanted to marry her, it was all ridiculous to her, but he wanted it. He seemed to think marriage would save her from this vindictive woman that still wanted revenge, even after all these years.

Marie started to wonder if she'd been cursed at birth. Her mother had an affair with a married man, unbeknownst to her, but still, Marie's father had been married. Of course, if what her mother had said during her frequent drunken ramblings was true, she'd only ensured she became pregnant to trap Nick anyway.

She'd had to live with her mother's hatred since her birth, with the vile venom that would not leave her mother's soul. She'd put up with it until the day her mother died. She'd thought that, at last, the curse was over. She'd been worried that Matteo would leave her, and there'd been worry over the bills, but there had been a part of her that felt... free.

She'd started to wonder about what else the world had to offer her, what life existed outside the parish borders, outside of the walls of this house. Matteo had crushed her hope, he'd shown her that her mother was right. All that existed outside of her home was wickedness. Evil. Malicious greed.

She stared up at the ceiling, a ceiling that she would soon have to leave, and knew that what she needed to do was calm down. She was overreacting and what she needed to do was calm down.

Marie pushed herself up from the floor and wandered into the kitchen. She took out a bowl of ice, wrapped a few blocks in a kitchen towel, and sat down at the table. It was too quiet in the almost empty house, so she reached over to turn on the old radio. She would take that with her when she left the house, she decided.

And where would she go? She had no family that would take her in. There were no friends that would allow her to crash on their couch. None that she thought were close enough to ask that favor of.

She'd have to see what was left from the sale... but then she thought about what Matteo had said. She would have to use whatever she had left from the sale to pay off his aunt. It would never cover what her mother owed the vengeful bitch in New York. Fuck!

Marie tossed the towel full of ice at the kitchen sink

with an angry shout, her mind in a panicked whirl. What could she do? What could she possibly do?

She could take whatever money was left and run far away, maybe. Run away to Vegas or somewhere in the California mountains, as long as it was far away. Would Matteo's aunt have him hunt her down?

Matteo had never said he was a part of the Mafia. He'd certainly never explained his work life but she wasn't stupid. The kind of money her mother had borrowed didn't come from a hotel mogul or a billionaire prince exiled to America. No, that money had come from the Mafia or a drug lord of some kind. Even a drug lord with that kind of money to throw around would have to be in some kind of gang or the Mafia.

Distracted, not really paying attention, Marie prepared herself a cup of coffee in the old French press she'd found at a yard sale years ago. The kettle was on the stove, but she forgot all about it until the pressure of the boiling water drove out the steam and the kettle began to whistle. She reached over, without thought, and burned her hand when she grabbed up the metal handle.

The way she pulled her hand back flung the kettle across the kitchen floor and hot boiling water poured out everywhere. "Fuck!"

She grabbed the towel that covered blocks of ice from the sink for her burned hand, picked up a potholder with the other, and grabbed up the kettle from the floor. With a resigned sigh, she put the kettle back onto the stove, turned off the radio, and went to bed.

She made do with a bottle of water from the fridge and turned on the television.

Her mind still raced, thoughts coming and going like bats hunting in the darkness, flitting from place to place. She could marry him, take him for whatever he was worth, and get on with her life. That was a plan. One she might be able to live with. If she could talk some of the softness out of her soul.

She knew she was weak, too soft for her own good. It wasn't all her mother's doing, Marie was naturally biddable. She wanted to keep the peace, wanted to sail through life without anyone else telling her she was worthless. Marie had never seen that as a bad thing, but now she saw that she had to harden herself up, just a little, if she wanted to get through this life unscathed.

Besides, even now, knowing that he'd betrayed her, that he'd used her, she wanted to feel his heat beside her. She wanted to be in his arms again to feel his kiss, his touch. She curled up into herself, a pillow tucked into her abdomen and wondered what the fuck was wrong with her.

Was she some kind of masochist, wanting to be punished for things she hadn't done? Was that what her mother had taught her, to take abuse and thrive despite, maybe because, of it? No, she wasn't that kind of person, she knew that. She just had... very bad luck. Luck that came about because of her mother's behavior.

All those years ago, Ruby had set in motion so many things, her own downfall included. Marie was still paying the price for those decisions, and she probably would for a long time. Should she just give in to Matteo's offer then?

Her eyes stared into the room, lit only by the television. It felt like a prison cell and always had. She could admit that to herself now. She'd always felt trapped and he'd offered her a way out. Alright, he'd lied to her about it, well, he hadn't really lied.

He'd left things out. He'd pretended he hadn't known her though, and that was a lie, wasn't it? Did it matter though, really?

Matteo could give her a life she'd never dreamed of, the kind of life her mother had coveted beyond reason. For once in her life, she could live without worry. If she gave in to Matteo's request, if she ignored the things he'd done to win her over, if he actually wanted to have some kind of relationship with her, then maybe she should consider his proposal?

He had been kind to her after all. He'd arranged to make sure she had free nights and had been there with her during the final stages of her mother's illness. He hadn't shied away, he'd supported her. That may have all been an act, a way to enlist her trust, but he'd done it. She'd seen the compassion on his face so many times, seen the way he'd tried to help her.

And then there was the way he kissed her. Surely a man couldn't fake that much desire? Sure, her mother would say that a man didn't care what he fucked as long as it laid still, but he kissed her with heat, with desire, a passion that wasn't like anything her mother had ever described. He held her to him. Touched her to bring her pleasure, not just himself.

He'd given her so much pleasure, in so many ways. Surely all of that hadn't been faked. Some of it must be real? Could she use that?

She hated herself for that thought. Could she use his feelings against him, that was something her mother would think, she knew.

Marie rolled the other way and wanted nothing more than to go back to his house and climb into bed with him. Damn, maybe she was a glutton for punishment. But was it really that delirious to hope for some happiness in life? To hope that maybe the world had something wonderful to offer to her?

Memories flashed in her mind, that night they'd spent together, wrapped up in each other. She could still remember the way he'd groaned her name and it made something... *twinge* inside of her. Deep inside, in that secret place that only Matteo had ever touched.

She had to admit it, even knowing that he'd betrayed her, with a pain in her heart that she couldn't ignore - she still wanted the man. She wanted to be near him, to smell him, and to hear the soft way he breathed when he was asleep. Was it so stupid to love him?

He was undoubtedly trouble, and even with all of that Mafia money, there could be legal consequences to a relationship with him. Could she stand that, if he was taken off to prison one day, or killed by a rival? No, she doubted the Mafia was anything like that nowadays. They'd modernized, surely.

But would they?

She reached over to her nightstand, dug around inside of the drawer, and found the bottle of pills there. She didn't want to take another one of the stupid things, but she needed to sleep. She needed to forget all of this. She was wandering off into impossibly ridiculous realms and it was time to let it go.

She'd wake up in the morning, make a decision, and then take the consequences as they came. She popped a single sleeping pill into her mouth, uncapped her bottle of water, and swallowed it down with a long drink. She put the bottle down, turned off the television, and accepted the darkness for what it offered.

In the darkness, there was no truth, no thought, just blackness that drew her into its waiting arms. She snorted and wondered if her sudden poetic bent was down to the pills or her emotional state. The rustle of the covers as she pulled them further up her neck was somehow as reassuring as the darkness. It was a familiar sound that meant she was wrapped in pure cotton sheets and a comforter that kept her warm.

It was a unique feeling at this time of year. The air conditioner kept her room cool, cool enough to need the comforter, something she'd never experienced in her life during the hot Louisiana nights. Not until after her mother's death, that is. Not until she'd spent the night at Matteo's home.

She could crank the air conditioner up until the damned thing froze now, either way, she wouldn't have to worry about the power bill. She would have to worry about getting out of bed though, and now that the pill was kicking in, that wasn't something she wanted to do.

Her eyelids became heavy, and she stretched out a leg to relieve the weight on her hips. A final sniffle and her eyes closed completely. She was done with this day, with her own thoughts, and fell into a dreamless sleep with a sigh she didn't even know she sighed. Tomorrow would come soon enough, decisions would have to be made, but for now, she was only going to sleep.

5

The smell of bacon and eggs lingered in the air, a reminder of the breakfast she'd made herself, as Marie left the house. She didn't look back or glance around to search out memories, she closed the door and walked to the car.

Matteo might be at home, she wasn't sure, but if he wasn't, she would wait for him. The logical thing to do would be to call him, but she was afraid that she'd change her mind or that he'd say something that would make her walk away. This was the only real "out" she'd been offered. She had to take it.

The obvious answer was to run far away, to get away from all of them. Leave the bill collectors and Matteo and his vengeful aunt behind, but she couldn't. She didn't want to live on the run, always looking over her shoulder, afraid to answer the phone or open mail, always working to stay one step ahead.

Which meant the best thing - the only thing - she

could do was take his offer. If she wanted to be cynical about it, she knew that she could stay married to him long enough for the debt to be cleared, divorce him with a nice alimony payment in tow, and get on with her life. Or, maybe, just maybe, he'd been a little bit honest with her. Maybe some of the adoration she'd seen in his eyes was real.

Her fingers tightened on the steering wheel as she pressed her foot down harder on the gas pedal. She couldn't afford to look at it that way, though, or to hope. That path would lead her only to folly, to the same kind of heartache that left a trail of disillusioned ex-wives with twisted lips and hateful eyes scattered along the edges. Nope, best not to even think the word "love".

Even if the whole idea of marriage nowadays was to seal the deal and offer the world proof that you were in love. Well, that and to make sure Uncle Sam didn't take more taxes from you than he should. No, cynicism might be sneered at by so many, but after her life, it was practical to be cynical. It was safe.

And all that Marie wanted in the world, all that she craved as her world crumbled around her, was safety. She wanted to be able to buy a new dress without worrying if she'd be able to eat the next week. She wanted to not be afraid of assassination, and she had to guess that was a very real possibility if she ran away. You didn't mess with Mafia people, not unless you wanted to get burned.

Even her mother hadn't left that world behind unscathed. Sure, Ruby had left her debt to her daughter, but she'd paid the price when Nick died. She'd lost everything, and for what? Stupidity and a daughter she never wanted.

One of John Lennon's songs came on through her phone, and she had to quickly shuffle it away. His pain at how much his mother hadn't wanted him, how his father had abandoned him, stung far too close to home. She'd put it on the phone because she *did* like it, but it was a song she only listened to when she felt at her strongest.

The tires of her car crunched along the driveway as she came to a stop in front of Matteo's house. "House", she scoffed to herself silently, mansion more like. She looked up at the white façade, the promise of luxury and opulence conveyed by the exterior - a promise that was kept inside. She'd wandered the halls, the rooms, and found only luxurious extravagance. Now, she was on the verge of being able to live in a house like that.

She had barely even switched off the car engine when Matteo swept out of the front door, but he paused on the top step. He stood there, taking in the car in his driveway. She looked back at him through the open window and felt her pulse race in her throat. He looked so handsome, so… expectant. It made her heart race a little harder and she could all but hear the blood as it rushed by her ears.

With unsteady fingers, she pushed the door open and got out of the car to stand by it. The driveway wasn't exactly the place she'd expected to have this conversation, but it was private. That lurking hulk of an employee that he had wouldn't be able to hear them, and she could get back in her car and drive away if it got too sketchy.

She put her hand up, her fingers splayed, to greet him.

Slowly, he came down the steps, and she admired him behind her cheap sunglasses. Dark blue jeans sculpted his muscles perfectly, and the white knit top he had on hugged him just right. His body was gorgeous, took her breath away, but it was his face, his mouth, and his silvery-gray eyes, that held her captive.

"Hi," he said simply as he came to stand in front of her, his hands in his pockets as he took her in. He looked like a teenager that was groveling out an apology and all she wanted to do was take him in her arms.

He'd lied to her, allowed her to depend on him, to fall in love with him. She couldn't give in to her body's response to him, no matter how strong the urge was. She pushed her sunglasses back up her sweat-slickened nose and looked down at herself.

She had on a pair of cheap jeans, a thin black long-sleeved shirt, and her ever-present flip flops. She didn't look like a million bucks, but she didn't care. She wanted to get this over with. She stiffened her neck, pretending to be unscathed so that she could speak without a quiver in her voice, "Hi."

She took a deep breath and leaned back against the car, trepidation hammering at her nerves. What did she say?

"I'm sorry, Marie," he said softly, so softly she almost missed it.

"Don't be," her head turned away from him as she told a lie she didn't want to speak. "It's not like I thought any of this was real."

"But… it was." He sighed. "Most of it. Some of it."

"Whatever." Her arms came up over her breasts, to

ward him off or to protect her heart from him, she wasn't sure which. "Look, you know what position I'm in, so if you want a wife you've bought, then I can only agree, right? I just need a little time to get used to the idea."

"How much time?" he asked quickly, perhaps afraid she'd change her mind if he delayed in answering. He hadn't looked at her either. He'd just stood there with his hands in his pockets, his eyes on that monstrosity of a house. The sunlight that glared from it made him squint and she wondered where his sunglasses were.

"A month?" She paused, licked suddenly dry lips, and took a breath. "I don't plan to ever do this again, so I'd like to find a decent dress. My debts, my mother's debts, will be cleared after this, right?"

"They will, I'll pay them myself. Even my aunt will be paid off." He sounded tired now as if his own plot burdened him in some way. Guilt, remorse, was that what she heard, she wondered.

"I don't have to meet her, do I?" Another barely spoken question, but one she had to know the answer to.

"Who?" His eyebrows came down in confusion, but he still didn't look at her. She didn't look at him either, but she could see the frown from the side of her eyes.

"Your aunt, the woman that's caused this?" She waved her hands in the air and turned to face him at last. "If she'd have just left well enough alone, I'd be destitute, but at least I wouldn't be sprawled on the barrel you have me over."

She wasn't sure where this assertive person she'd suddenly become had come from, but she was going with it. It was probably sheer bravado, she thought but didn't care.

"If your mom hadn't," he started. The immediate glare that the beginning of that sentence caused stopped him. "If my uncle hadn't…"

"It doesn't matter who started that crap all those years ago, she decided to carry it on. She decided that tormenting a dying woman was a fun way to get her jollies. Well, she's fucked me over, so I hope she's happy. The feud continues."

"Let's not argue, Marie," he sighed out and turned to her. "We'll be down here for a month more, at least, but then I have to get back to New York. We have to get back to New York. You might meet her, you might not, I don't know. But I'll be there, so you'll be safe."

"Fine." She didn't have a whole lot more to say to him, so she leaned back against her car again. "Is that all?"

"I'll need some paperwork from you, and we'll have to apply for a marriage license together. So, we should meet up once you've decided on a dress. Oh, here, use this to buy whatever you want." He moved towards her, pulled out his wallet, and took out a credit card.

She stared at it, at the name on the card, and felt her heart seize up. Whatever she wanted? She wanted to buy his love, to be his love, she didn't want that stupid card. For a moment, she almost ran away, but then she remembered that stack of bills on her kitchen table. She might even be able to save the house if he was going to pay off the debts she now owed. Her hand shook slightly as she took the card and slid it into her back pocket.

"Thanks." That was all because she couldn't think of what else to say.

"I'll wait for your call then." He stopped and turned to her. "Let me know if you need anything else."

"I will." She turned to open her car door. "See you later."

"Indeed, you will, Marie," his deep voice promised. She looked at him as she slid into her car seat and turned the engine over. He didn't seem like the chastened schoolboy anymore, he looked like a grown man with plans to make her his.

She swallowed and decided it wouldn't be a good idea to ask him about her wifely duties yet. His eyes told her there was one duty he was still very much interested in.

She put the car in drive, despite her body's demand to go back to him, and sped down the drive. Rocks from the graveled surface flew out behind the car as she raced away, but she didn't care about the damage those rocks might do. She had to get away, otherwise, she'd make a fool out of herself.

Her thoughts froze as she drove down the road, her movements were automatic. She made it home in one piece, and let herself into the quiet house. She went to the coffee pot and turned it on. She needed the jolt it would give her. She flipped on the radio and waited for the gurgle to tell her the coffee had brewed.

She had a month, at the most, before he expected her to go to New York with him. There was business down here, he'd said, and she had to wonder what that business was. Was it drugs? More than likely it was something to do with gambling.

Her mom used to go on about mobsters and how Marie needed to stay away from Mafia boys. Well, it was more than obvious that she'd failed to avoid those kinds of boys. She'd fallen in love with one at the first opportunity.

She wanted to be greedy, to think about all of the things that she could buy now, but that wasn't what had drawn her to Matteo. It was his eyes, the way he'd treated her. Would that change now?

Thoughts spun around in her brain so fast that they made her head pound. She didn't want to think about money, she didn't want to think that her only interest in Matteo had ever been about the poverty he could take her away from. It was sensible though, he had money, he'd never hidden that fact. His ability to lift her out of the life of abuse she'd endured had appealed, more than his money, however.

Where her mother had only offered her misery and hate, Matteo had offered her love, friendship, and joy. He'd brought light to her dark world. So, no, it wasn't all about his money. It was more about the fact that he made her feel human.

She poured milk into a mug filled with the fresh coffee and sat back down at the table. She looked at the stack of bills before she looked away. She didn't have to worry about those anymore. Matteo would take care of them. She didn't have to worry about anything really, other than meeting his witch of an aunt.

That she didn't want to do. Marie knew the meeting would be tense, after all, Marie was the product of the woman's husband's infidelity. She was proof that he hadn't really loved her. How could it go right?

No, she'd marry him, and later, after the bills were paid and the house was hers, she could divorce him. If she wanted to. Maybe he'd be a good husband, maybe this wasn't all some game he was playing with his aunt. Why would he want to marry her otherwise, really? She was a nobody, she didn't bring him anything but debt, so perhaps there was a part of him that really did want to marry her? How else could she explain it?

That's what she'd do then, she'd marry him and get on with her life. After the divorce, she could do whatever she wanted: travel, find out who she really was after all these years of living with her mother's torture. She'd learned over the last few days that waking up with the knowledge that her mother was no longer around to tell her how terrible she was, what a burden she was, how the world would be better without her, was really… nice.

She felt another pang of guilt, but she was coming to live with those. Her mother had been horrible to her for her entire life, Marie was perfectly aware of that. She'd become used to it, even if it got to her some days. Now, though, she had a chance at so much more than just existing. She had a chance to live, to live a life she'd never dreamed of, and she'd take that chance. It wasn't like she had any other options.

6

Matteo walked back into his office as he heard her drive away and sat down at his computer. She'd left angry, hurt, and on the verge of tears. He knew that, yet he couldn't, wouldn't, do anything to make it stop. He wanted her, had to have her, and with his aunt in the way, this was the only way he could do it.

His aunt was not one that he would normally fuck around with. That was before he met Marie, before he felt... something. Emotions weren't his normal playing ground, he didn't have them, not really, but from the moment he'd seen Marie in that parking lot, he knew he had to have her.

Now, after a long tormenting wait, when he thought he'd go mad wanting her, he'd had her. That should have got her out of his system, but it didn't. It made him want her even more. He wanted to own those sighs of hers, the way she arched her back and twisted her hips. He wanted all of that, all of her, to be his. The problem was... his aunt.

The only way he could think of to get around that problem was to marry her. He'd made the offer to Marie, an offer he knew she'd have to accept, knowing that it would hurt her. The fact that he had to tell her his aunt wanted what was owed to her would hurt her anyway, he figured he'd soften that blow with… marriage. It would take care of her debts and she'd be his wife.

Women all over the world wanted to be his wife. They'd thrown themselves at him since he was 13. He knew women wanted the power that would be his one day, the wealth. Marie had never wanted any of that, she'd only wanted to be his. Now, she needed money, and it was the one thing that would get him what he wanted, what she wanted.

A chance to get each other out of their systems. They could divorce, even if the church would frown on it. Matteo was not a religious man, despite his upbringing, and Marie wasn't religious either. If, when, they grew tired of each other, they could divorce and get on with their lives.

Simple enough, he told himself. He took a cigar out of a box he kept in a drawer of his desk and went out to the pool. The first place he'd made her come. The night replayed in his mind, the way she'd clung to him, the incredible sounds she'd made, the wonder in her eyes as he got her off. It made him hard just to think about it, and he hoped she wouldn't make him wait the entire month he'd offered her.

He wanted to fly her off to Vegas or anywhere else that would allow them to be married that day so that he would know she was his, and only his, right then. But she needed to come around to this. He'd seen the hard way she'd held herself away from him and saw it for what it was - a play to look strong.

She didn't have that shell yet, not the one that so many people he knew had. That amazed him because she'd grown up with a mother that was terrible to her, abusive to the point that Marie probably should have been taken away from her long before her mother even became ill. That she had no defense other than to shrink into herself was amazing.

He'd seen the start of that shell today, that was for sure. The fair thing for Marie would be if she didn't have to actually grow that shell to protect herself, but he knew that she'd need it to be his wife. She'd have to learn to defend herself from others, to stand apart and away from them. Especially with his aunt.

Celeste would have an absolute fit when she found out what he'd done, but for once in his life, he'd decided to defy the woman that took him from his mother. He'd decided to defy the woman that would give him her empire, even if it cost him that empire because he didn't just want Marie and her sweet innocence, he craved her.

It would not do to let her know that, but she would probably guess it from his little act of defiance. He was certain she had some nice Italian girl, a good, Catholic, Italian girl in mind for him when the time came, but this time, he wanted something, someone, of his own. Only his.

Marie would need time to become accustomed to his needs, to become used to the idea that she'd been blackmailed into being his bride, but with time she'd come around. If that shell she was growing didn't become too hard. If he could protect her from most of his aunt's wrath, and the spitefulness of the women in his world, as well as the worry that came with his life choices, then he'd get to have the woman he'd come to adore.

He didn't want Marie to turn into the kind of wife that most of his friends had, tough as nails, brash, and ready to fight at a moment's notice. He wanted the inquisitive, intelligent woman that wanted to know more about the world, the delicate creature that stepped out with wonder every time he was with her. He wanted to protect her, and that was scary at first.

He'd kept her at arm's length for a very long time, not because of his aunt's order, but because he'd known instinctively that Marie was dangerous for him. She was the kind of woman you fall in love with, and he wasn't sure he was capable of that. If he deserved that. In fact, if it had been left up to him, he'd have gone home the moment he met her. He didn't want to destroy what she was or taint it.

The voice of his aunt played in the back of his mind the entire time telling him he had to do what she asked, and he'd done it. Now, he'd paid the price: he'd hurt her and she'd withdrawn from him. She'd come around, he hoped.

If not, he'd find a way to bring the wonder back to her eyes. That was the one thing that had hurt him the most when she'd stepped out of her car earlier. The wonder was gone. In its place was a dead stare, one that bore witness to a soul in torment. She felt like a commodity to be traded, and he couldn't blame her for that. To protect her from his aunt, though, he had to do this.

He'd suspected his aunt was insane for a very long time, even if he'd never admit it to anyone, not even his mother. He barely admitted it to himself. This obsession with Ruby Hebert proved it. Now, her obsession had switched over to Marie and he couldn't stand the idea of the young woman being hurt more than she already had been.

This wouldn't get him through the day, he decided and left the office to change into a pair of slacks and a black shirt. Paired with soft, black leather loafers, he looked the part of a man with wealth and good taste, the image his aunt had taught him to always present to the world. He was a man with power, that could give and take life with a mere word, though he didn't want to bring Marie into that part of his world. He hoped she'd never ask him about the more violent side of his life. He didn't know how honestly he'd be able to answer her.

He wasn't proud of all of the things he'd done in his life, but he'd had to prove himself to his aunt and to the people that served him. He'd had to be brutal on more than one occasion, and he'd do it again if he had to. That was the life that had been handed to him by Celeste.

He went out to the car, the car that Ruby hadn't even been able to see because she was bedridden, and looked at it. It had been updated, sure, but it was still the same car that Marie's parents had been in the day her father died. His uncle, by marriage, had died in this car and for a moment, he wondered if it was haunted.

He pushed that thought away with a shiver of disquiet.

He didn't want to think about that anymore. Instead, he started the car and drove out to the highway. A truck passed him by, and he gave the two-finger flick that seemed to be required from most drivers down in this part of the world.

Back home people avoided eye contact and giving a flick of the hand like that might be seen as a threat. You just didn't do it. But down here, he'd caught on to the habit of returning the flicks that were a simple courtesy. It was a statement that could mean "I see you", or "have a nice day", he didn't know but it was… nice.

He realized he felt different down here. Oh, he was still the same man his aunt sent to terrify a woman into paying an old debt, but he was also a tiny bit different now. He liked how relaxed people seemed, like they weren't always on guard for threats, as if they didn't worry about pick-pockets and those that meant to do them harm.

He'd found a few things annoying, but even that annoyance was tempered by the charm of watching two women stand in the middle of an aisle discussing their children's after-school activities. He'd learned that he might have to answer questions that would never cross the mind of people up north to ask. Like how he was. A lot of people asked him how he was doing today, and it was far more pleasant than he'd thought it would be.

He knew he'd miss that once he got back to New York, and that made him wonder how Marie would deal with it. Although, if he had his way, he'd keep her far too busy to worry about being homesick. She'd get used to living up there if he decided that's where they would stay. And if his aunt did finally hand over the family business to him, he would keep them up there.

He drove to a derelict parking lot and stopped the car. It was a strip club, but you wouldn't know that from the outside. The building was painted black, there were no windows, and the sign out front was off. He knew what it was, though, his source had arranged a meeting there.

The club was not the kind of place he'd have chosen to hold a meeting but the man that he was about to meet was eager to impress. A strip club was far from anything that would impress Matteo, but the man didn't seem to know that. He walked into the club, saw a woman on the stage, barely covered in a tiny bikini, her body upside down on a pole.

She was an attractive blond, but she didn't have the appeal of Marie, not even close. He ordered a drink from the bartender and found a seat. He thought about Marie, about the things he wanted to teach her now that they were lovers. He wanted to introduce her to things he knew she'd never dreamed of, but most of all, he wanted to own her, body and soul.

He wouldn't be rough with her, that wasn't what he was after, and he'd never physically harm her, but he wanted… more. He knew she'd give it too, once she'd had time. He felt his pulse race and his skin heat up as he thought about her, and cleared his throat. Now wasn't the time to think about that, he reminded himself.

Later, when he was alone, he could think about all the ways he'd please her. And the many ways she could please him.

"Mr. Mazza?" He heard a man ask, and looked around to find an overweight man dressed in a cheap suit behind him.

Randall Metrejean was the king of illegal gambling in the state, which was something in a state where most forms of gambling were legal, if tightly controlled. It wasn't those illegal gambling dens that Matteo was necessarily interested in, though. He wanted in on the legal stuff as well.

"That's me, Randall." He'd only spoken to the man on the phone, but he had a file on him with a picture to identify him by. The man had more money than the state had in its coffers, but he wore cheap suits, drove a car that was falling apart, and lived in a double-wide on the outskirts of New Orleans, all to keep the heat off himself.

The law knew about him, there was no doubt of that, but he also had the law on his side. In his pocket, to be exact. Matteo needed those connections to get started down here. He had already had several gambling machines sent down here to use in the casino he wanted to open, disguised as an ice cream parlor. It was Randall that would help Matteo to get the permits he'd need to open a legal casino.

Matteo didn't want to think about it too much, but it was more than gambling that would go on in that ice cream parlor. Those machines would dispense far more than coins for his clients, but he wasn't ready to talk to anyone about that yet.

"Have a seat. Would you like a drink?" Matteo waved at

the bartender and then at a chair as the wide man sat down. He wasn't a very tall man, but he was… wide.

Randall plunged a hand with thick fingers through stringy black hair and looked at the stage. "Now that's a sight worth waking up early for. Nicky sure is a fine woman."

Matteo attempted to hide the sneer that threatened to mar his features. A man that knew the names of the dancers on the stage was very sad, in Matteo's opinion. Surely, a man in Randall's position would have better things to do than hang around strip clubs.

"I'm sure she is." Matteo paused while Randall asked the bartender for a beer. "Now, I'd like to get right down to business…"

"Wait a minute, wait a minute. Let me watch the end of Nicky's show."

Matteo closed his mouth and turned his face away so the sad little man wouldn't see the way he rolled his eyes. He'd much rather be at home, dreaming about Marie and their wedding night, but business came first. He'd dream about her later.

7

Marie took the tea-length silk dress from the hanger on her closet door and pulled the side zipper down. With a deep breath, she stepped into the dress before she pulled it up over her body. She'd found it in a second-hand shop in New Orleans; the perfect dress for the perfect sham wedding.

It was all arranged and today was the day. They'd go to the courthouse for a short ceremony, and then they'd be on their way. There wasn't really even a reason she should wear the dress, other than it was her first wedding. She looked in the mirror as she pulled the side zipper up and the material stretched snugly across her breasts.

The silk hid the new underwear she'd bought, all white lace and pure. A sham, really, but it was tradition, right? Marie sat down on the bed to pull up white stockings and to slide on the white stiletto heels she'd bought to go with the dress.

It wasn't an overly fancy dress at all. The neckline was

square, with two wide shoulder straps to hold the bodice up. It fit snugly down her torso before it flared out at her hips, all the way down to her calves. A crinoline beneath puffed the skirt out and made it… pretty. That was the word she thought as she glanced in the mirror.

She'd twisted her hair up into a French twist at the back of her head, and put on a small pillbox hat with a short net for a veil. She looked like the perfect 1950s bride. Perhaps an odd choice, but that was kind of how she felt. Trapped in a world of beauty, manners, and old-fashioned expectations. But… pretty.

An arranged marriage was nothing more than that, wasn't it? A pretty sham of what should be. A prison that a woman with no money of her own could not escape.

Would they still have the passion, though? She wondered about that as she applied a light layer of makeup to her face, just enough to highlight the features the woman at the shop had taught her. Would he still want her in his bed?

Uncertainty filled her as she got up from the bed. Did she want Matteo to touch her, to have sex with her? Or did she want to be left alone to fully encase her heart in ice in peace? She'd thought about it for two weeks now but there was still no answer. She simply didn't know what she wanted.

She'd simply done what she needed to do to get through the dreadful days and the tormenting nights. She'd wanted so much from Matteo, but it wasn't really that much. Not really. She'd wanted his love, nothing more. She didn't care about money, or about the things he could give her. All she wanted was to matter, to love him, and be loved in return.

Instead, she was going to be his property for all intents and purposes. Something he'd bought and that hurt her deeply. The burning ache of that hurt made her want to run, to just take his credit card and run as far as she could before he reported the card stolen. Honesty was something that came naturally to her, however, and the thought of lying to Matteo hurt almost more than this forced marriage did.

Even if he had lied to her.

With one last glance behind her, Marie left her childhood home, now empty of the possessions she wanted to take with her and placed in a bedroom at Matteo's. She would have her own bedroom, she suspected that was because he knew she would need her own space.

The wedding itself was a blur, words were spoken, papers signed, and before she knew it, they were being congratulated by three people she didn't even know. They'd needed two witnesses and those had been chosen from the staff at the courthouse. Not the wedding Marie might have envisioned, nothing like it at all, but it was done, and she was now Matteo's wife.

She glanced over at him as they walked out of the courthouse and felt her heart lurch in her chest. She still loved him, then. Her heart couldn't help but love him, even if her head screamed that she was insane and shouldn't love, or trust, him.

He was dressed tastefully, in a tailored dark blue suit with a white shirt and a silky pink tie that he must have chosen for the wedding. His hair was cut perfectly, just long enough to run her fingers through, something they ached to do, but she held herself back. He'd tricked her, used her, and now he'd forced her to marry him.

And for what? To protect her from his miserable aunt's schemes as he'd said?

That didn't make any sense. If he'd been sent down here to humiliate and ruin Ruby even further, why try to protect her? Did he care about her? Was that it?

He'd said as much, but she hadn't believed him. There must be some ulterior motive here, other than love. Maybe he'd married her because his aunt had chosen a mate for him and he didn't like the woman? If he was that under her thumb then it might be possible. But then, by marrying her he was defying her, so maybe not?

It was all too confusing and too much to think about right now, so she focused on the bright sky. There were a few clouds up there, but other than that, it was a clear day, lovely for a wedding really.

"I'll meet you at the house, shall I?" His voice broke into her thoughts and she turned to him, a blank look on her face.

"Of course, if that's what you wish." She wouldn't argue, she didn't have the strength to, not really.

"Be careful." He leaned in, brushed a tender kiss along her cheek, and left to get into his car.

Some wedding, she thought as she climbed into her own car. That was the most… boring kiss he'd ever given her. That kiss was also the saddest one he'd ever given her.

Even he knew this was wrong, but he had it in his head that it was necessary.

Tears stung at her eyes but she swiped them away carefully, she didn't want to smudge the makeup she'd only learned to apply so recently. This emptiness would be her life now, this sadness would always be with her until she could find a way to get out of this marriage of convenience. Or whatever it was, she couldn't decide.

He'd forced her into it - it was an arranged marriage and it was a marriage of convenience. Not so easy to define, yet it all came down to the same thing, she was now his wife. And he was her husband.

They hadn't spoken a lot over the last couple of weeks, just texts about the wedding, a short meeting where she brought him the papers he needed to pay the bills she now owed, and to apply for the marriage license. They hadn't discussed what he expected from her after the ceremony, or how long this sham was supposed to last.

They were questions she wanted to ask him, but even as she stepped into the house a short while later, something held her back. She thought she might be afraid of the answers he gave, or that the questions might make him angry. As a new wife, a wife who barely knew who her husband really was, she didn't want to rock the boat too much.

"I'm in the dining room, Marie," he called out to her and she followed the sound of his voice, slowly. Each step was like the tolling of a bell, a bell that pronounced her doom.

"Hello," she said softly as she came in and saw a full

meal on the table. It was barely lunchtime, but the cook had obviously been busy.

"Have a seat, Marie, and eat. You look pale." He directed her to the chair beside him.

"Thank you." She ate quietly, the spicy heat of the seafood jambalaya the only thing she noticed about the meal. She drank the crisp glass of green wine he poured for her and then poured herself another.

She heard him set down his silverware and she looked up to see he swiped at his mouth with a red linen napkin. He'd finished his meal, now what?

His hand came out, took her hand, and turned it so that her palm faced up. His fingers stroked at the pulse point in her wrist, and she took a deep breath to try to steady the way that pulse raced. The question he asked changed everything about that moment, made her pulse race even harder.

"Do you trust me at all, Marie, after what I've made you do?" His eyes were cloaked behind a mask of curiosity, but some hint in his voice, some warning, made her body respond instantly with hot desire.

He still wanted that from her then.

"I'm not sure, Matteo. I trust you with my body, of course, but the rest of me? I don't know." Always honest, even if it made his eyes tense at the corner.

The tension disappeared behind a smile, a seductive smile, meant to put her at ease. It made her body tense with excitement, but not fear. That was the domain of her heart, and that she quickly put behind a wall.

His fingers moved, left her sensitive skin before he

stood up and shut the dining-room door. "It's our wedding day, Marie, time to celebrate it the best way we know how."

He pulled her up from her seat and she followed him as he moved down the table, to a place that was free of the dishes. "Bend over."

She wanted to protest, she wanted to ask him for more than a quick fuck in the dining room, but she didn't question it. She was his now, and he wanted to prove it. Instinct told her that.

Without a word, she bent over the table and gasped at the coolness of the varnished wood. The soft rustle of silk against cotton caught her attention and she wondered if he was undressing.

"Give me your hands." It wasn't a question, but a demand. Her body responded with liquid heat that surged in her veins, straight to points she now wanted him to touch.

Somewhere, a part of her wanted to protest, wanted to say it wasn't supposed to be like this, but another part was excited about the way he'd taken control. A bigger part of her wanted his attention however it came and would drop her to her knees if it meant he touched her.

She moved her hands behind her back and tried to settle on the table comfortably. Something pulsed from her chest, straight down between her thighs, when she felt the silk of his tie wrap around her wrists. The bond wasn't tight, but she wouldn't be able to break free if she wanted to.

There was a hint of danger there, in being bound, bent

over a table, and at his mercy. Still, she wasn't afraid. She was… aroused. Curious. Eager for more.

And also, very fucking confused.

Her body was in overdrive and her brain went quiet as his fingers let go of hers and moved down her body. The way she was bent over pushed the crinoline out, her lower half must have been on display to him, but she didn't care. She was hungry for his touch, suddenly, starving for it.

They'd only slept together once before the wedding, but her body had remembered his touch every day since. In her dreams, he touched her, loved her, made her scream his name, and now he was there. He stepped away slightly, paused, and she knew he was looking at her.

What a picture she must make: her skirt pushed up by the crinoline, her bottom covered in silky lace, the garters that held up her white stockings on display for only him. Only for Matteo. She was his wife, and he was about to make it legally so.

"Matteo," she murmured quietly, but he shushed her.

The sound of his belt being loosened, the slow way his zipper came down, and the sound as his pants fell to the floor made her want to slide her panties out of the way just enough for him to slide into her, she was so eager for him. "Please."

That was all, nothing more, just a please, but it held so many other words. Please fuck me, please make me come, please end this torment.

He ignored that plea and knelt behind her. She heard the sound as his knees hit the floor. Felt the way his hands opened her flesh to him, brushed the fabric of her barely-there panties aside. She heard him groan as his lips brushed over her folds, just enough to gather the taste of her on his mouth, to smell her desire.

His tongue came out to taste her more fully, to gather her liquid desire to savor. He sucked at his own tongue for a moment before he moved back in, using his hands to move her thighs wider apart so that he could dive deeper into her flesh. The press of his thumbs on her ass was almost painful, almost too much, but at the same time, that sensation of pain thrilled her, made her want more, and her hips rocked into his face.

She wanted more, needed more, but didn't dare ask for it. Not when she was at his mercy like this. He might decide to just fuck her and get it over with, and she would die if he did that.

Marie knew she was in no position to make demands right now. Some part of Matteo needed this moment, needed to seal their marriage in this way, and she'd agreed to it when she signed on the dotted line. What surprised her was how much she enjoyed his domination, how thrilled she was that he'd taken control. For once in her life, she didn't have to make a choice, she didn't have to make a decision. All she had to do was feel.

So she gave herself up to whatever it was he desired, whatever it was that this moment was, and let him have his way. She knew, deep down, that if she protested, he would let her up to go on her way, but she also knew that she didn't want to be left alone. She wanted him to fuck her, more than anything.

Right after he made her come, that is.

His tongue moved through her slick folds, seeking until he found that spot that made her moan helplessly. She tried to look back, to see what he was doing, but she couldn't. She moved her head on the table, but she couldn't see anything there either and decided to put a mirror in here the first chance she got to buy one. Maybe several.

She wanted to see him on his knees as he serviced her, as he lost himself in her taste.

His fingers gripped her tighter as her hips twitched again in response to the way his tongue danced on her clit. She forgot to breathe as he paused to suck at the throbbing nub and thought she'd faint. His tongue flicked at her again, danced in that drumming beat that made her quiver, and her lungs came back to life. She sucked in air, moaned his name, and wished she could bury her fingers in his hair.

She was trapped there, though, his to control, his to dominate, as he unleashed his desire on her. At that moment, she didn't care. The control he had over her actually made her body react more strongly. The sweet pain of his thumbs on her ass eased slightly as he moved one hand down while the other moved closer, to that place that no one else had ever touched. His thumb pressed into her there but didn't penetrate, and somehow that made it even more pleasurable, to feel his thumb press at her ass like that.

His other hand moved down, stopped just above his chin, and she came apart as two of his long fingers slid into her. A loud moan of surprised pleasure escaped her throat as her body clenched in a sudden release, clenched around his fingers, to suck him deeper inside of her.

Matteo didn't stop, he just kept right on going, as the waves ebbed, and then crashed over her all over again until she was little more than a pool of liquid that had no thought. Her brain turned off, became completely blank as the second wave rattled through her. She wasn't aware of anything except pleasure until she felt the glide of his cock along her folds.

He wanted to fuck her now, he wanted to be inside of her. His fingers were still inside when he pressed into her, making the entry of his cock all the tighter until it almost hurt. That is until his thumb pressed against the bud of her ass all over again. Her walls clenched around him then, dragged his fingers and his cock into her, sucked them in, until she heard him groan in absolute delight.

They didn't speak to each other. There was nothing really to say, their bodies did all the speaking for them. Matteo drove into her hard and fast, his fingers still there, still inside of her, on her, directing her.

She came apart all over again as he gave one final groan, a shout of completion, and she felt his pulse deep inside of her. He emptied himself into her completely, his fingers on her hips now, to hold her still as he flooded her with his pleasure. She didn't care, she was too amazed at the way her body tried to swallow him, at how good she felt, to care that his fingers were a little too rough, that his hips had slammed her into the edge of the table a little too hard. Those sensations only heightened the pleasure she felt as she surrendered to him completely.

They stayed there for a moment as their bodies came back down to earth. She expected him to say something, to say anything, but he didn't. She was still sprawled on the table, but when the moment passed and he didn't say anything she got up and turned to look at him. He didn't look at her, he just pulled up his pants and went back to sit down. He sipped at his wine, and something in her finally began to hurt. That's when he spoke again.

"Things will be a little different now, Marie." He finally looked up at her, those deep brown eyes clouded with something she didn't understand. "You're mine now, you see? Mine."

She opened her mouth, couldn't think of what to say, and stood up. Without a word, she left the room. She'd always been his, she thought as she climbed the stairs to her bedroom. Why didn't he see that?

8

———————

*L*ife goes on, Marie thought a few days later. She was in her old car and on her way into New Orleans for more shopping. Matteo wanted to buy her a new car, but she'd refused that, for now. The old Ford was a part of her life and always had been. Now clothes, that was a totally different matter.

She parked at a boutique and went inside. She had on a $300 blue silk dress that was slouchy at the top but fitted around her hips, a pair of black tights, and dark-brown, leather ankle boots. She looked the part, especially after she'd had her dark hair trimmed, shaped, and styled. Matteo wanted his wife to present an image that reflected well on him.

That's why she hadn't complained when he gave her a long list of clothes to buy with things she could buy and things she couldn't. He wanted her to look the part of a rich wife, right down to the manicure on her fingers and the earrings in her ears. She had no idea how much she'd spent so far, and he didn't seem to care.

She'd spotted a pair of boots at this boutique yesterday but hadn't had room to put any more bags in the car, so she'd decided to come back. She walked in and a blond, young woman came out, eager to please. Marie found it amusing now, how people were so eager to talk to her, eager to know more about her, especially back at home. People in the grocery store actually smiled at her once they'd heard about her marriage.

The woman at the bank had even said her name, Marie, instead of the usual "Miss" she called her. Marie put the fancy credit card down and sat down on the settee the woman directed her to. She tried on the boots she wanted, another pair, and two sweater dresses. She was buying clothes for their excursion to New York. It would be cold up there and she would need clothes for going out in, for staying home but expecting company in, and loungewear.

She had a dozen pairs of silk pajamas, nighties that were warm and some that were sexy, lingerie, shoes, and so much more than she'd ever owned before. She probably had more clothes than she'd ever owned, in total, throughout her life. She even had evening dresses that she wasn't sure she'd get to wear, but she owned them now.

On top of that, Matteo had paid all of the bills that were owed, and the house was hers, there if she ever wanted to go back to it. Something told her that she wouldn't, but he'd insisted she keep it, just in case. She'd planned to sell it, but maybe he was right. She might want to revisit it one day.

Marie finished her purchases and went to a small restaurant to get some lunch. Matteo told her when he left that morning that he wouldn't be back until late in the evening, so she knew she wouldn't leave him at home alone. Not that he minded being there alone, but she felt she should be with him if he was at home.

So far, things were... okay in their household. They didn't talk a lot, not like they used to, and Matteo had become a little rougher when it came to sex, but she didn't mind that. She reveled in it actually. He'd treated her like a doll when they first met, to be handled with a little more power, a little more control, was nice.

Outside of the bedroom, their life was different. He didn't tell her what to do, where to go, or who to talk to. He did control what she wore, but that was necessary. She had no head for fashion, and he had an image to uphold. If he wasn't the heir to her father's little Mafia ring, then he might not care if she continued to run around in shorts and flip flops, but he was.

Marie paused, a cup of coffee held stiffly in her hands, as a new idea occurred to her. She was the only child of Nick Alfonsi. Celeste had chosen Matteo because he was her nephew, no relation at all to Nick. Wasn't Marie entitled to some of that inheritance, though? Wasn't she the one that should be the head of this "family"?

The inner workings of such organizations weren't something Marie knew much about, her mother had hated anything to do with the Mafia, and that included books and movies. Most of that was fiction, anyway, but it would have given her an idea if nothing else. Celeste ran the business now, so it was apparent a woman could be the head of the family.

Marie knew why she wasn't, why Celeste had left her with her mother and taken her own blood relative in as the heir. She was the bastard daughter of an affair - illicit and illegitimate. She was a reminder of what Nick had done, and Celeste hadn't wanted her around. Which made her worry. What would she do when she found out Matteo had married the one woman that would be a constant reminder of what Nick had done?

That sent a chill down her spine, one so strong she nearly shivered in the warm café. Matteo would keep her safe, she knew he would. He'd become distant since their marriage, he didn't speak to her about a lot of things, he wasn't as curious about her as he used to be, but she suspected some of that was her own fault.

He had forced her into this and she resented it. She'd presented a cold front to him those first few days after he'd revealed the truth to her. Matteo was simply returning what she'd given off to him. They'd both warm up, given time. She didn't know if there would ever truly be love in their marriage, but there could be caring affection. There was certainly desire, by the buckets.

Would he ever take her seriously enough to let her help with the family business, she wondered? Once Celeste was gone, off to Italy or whatever her plans were, would Matteo let her have some say in what should be hers, anyway?

It was a new idea, intriguing even. If Celeste let her live, that is.

Marie gulped and took a sip of her coffee to calm her nerves. Maybe she should take some self-defense lessons. She'd try to talk to him about it all, at some point before they left. They had a little more time, so maybe not tonight.

She drove home with her purchases and carried them up to her bedroom. She still had her own room, and that was fine. She didn't sleep there, it was mainly a place for her to store her clothes, and she had her own bathroom over there. She'd go there sometimes, when Matteo was out, and read a book in bed, or have a nap, but she slept with him every night. He'd asked her to, after that first night after their wedding.

He liked to have her with him while he was asleep, he'd admitted with a red tint to his cheeks. He slept better. She hadn't pushed him away or laughed, she'd simply nodded her head in agreement and turned to spoon up against him. He could be sensitive at the most unexpected moments.

She put her purchases away, went down to find some packages had been delivered, and found several brand-new, designer suitcases big enough to hold most of her new wardrobe. They were all for her and more were on the way. She'd need them to pack all of her new clothes. This reminder that she would soon be leaving her hometown, a town she'd never left for long, brought on a quiet case of melancholia.

She went outside, now dressed in a pair of black yoga pants and a long flannel shirt that came down to her knees, and sat on the back patio with a cup of coffee. It was quiet here, as it had been at the house she grew up in. If you didn't count the sound of the wind in the trees and the call of animals in the distance.

Matteo had given her one answer when she asked him what it was like in New York - noisy. It drove him to distraction sometimes, he'd told her, back when they still had discussions. He'd grown up in that noise: the constant thrum of motor vehicles, people, machines, all of it came together to form some vibration of sound that was never, ever quiet, even in the most soundproofed homes. You could still hear the noise, he'd said.

Could she get used to that, she wondered? Where would she go if she couldn't? She watched the sunset and heard Matteo's car drive up a little after six o'clock. She stayed in her place, even though there was a chill in the air now. She wanted to absorb all the quiet that she could.

"Marie? What are you doing out here in the cold? Are you alright?" He came out to the porch, his deep-set eyes, powerful cheekbones, and that strong jaw of his beckoning her to him. He could blink at her sometimes and it would make her knees weak.

She turned away with a frown and sat back in her chair. "I'm enjoying the quiet while I can. I remembered what you said about New York when I saw all that luggage you ordered for me. About how noisy it is. How you can never get any peace, even in your own home."

"You get used to it," he started, but then shook his head ruefully. "No, that's not true. I think you just learn to cope with it. I don't think you ever really get used to it."

He sat down, poured coffee out of a carafe he'd brought out with him, then added cream. He held the carafe out to her and she shook her head no. "I've had my fill today, I think."

It was the most relaxed they'd been around each other since before her mother passed away. It was nice to have him back, and relaxed, if only for a little while.

"I will miss this when we go." His face was trained to the woods beyond the perimeter, lost in his own world. "It's so damn peaceful here."

"We can come back," she assured him and hoped she was right.

"We can, and that will make this place all the more special, won't it? We know we always have this to come back to when it becomes too much." He sighed and drank his coffee in silence.

She was ready to eat but decided she could wait. Let him enjoy what she'd spent the last couple of hours enjoying. She'd enjoy the peace that came from being near him, even if she didn't admit that to him.

9

The staff were all in their quarters by the time Marie and Matteo walked up the stairs to their bedroom. They each had their own small set of rooms and would go there in the evenings. It was one of the perks of working in the house; they didn't have to rent a place out if they didn't want to. There was the cook, two housekeepers, and the guy that answered the door that Marie suspected was more of a bodyguard/assistant/doorman. She avoided him, he just gave her the creeps with his watchful eyes and quietness.

They'd had dinner a few hours before and had sat down to watch a movie in the living room after. Marie had decided to go up to bed and Matteo followed along with her. She went to her room, grabbed a nightgown, then went back to her bathroom to have a shower.

"Marie, are you alright?" She heard him call out about five minutes after she got into the hot water to let the steam roll away the aches she'd accumulated throughout the day.

"Yeah," she called back, "just decided to have a shower before we go to sleep."

He didn't answer and she was about to turn the water off to ask if he was alright when he opened the door, completely naked and more than ready for her from the looks of him. She stepped back to let him in.

As usual, he was quiet as he looked at her. He filled his brain with wet images of her before he reached out to tip her head back. His kiss was hungry, wild, and she let herself go as he forced her jaw open with a thumb against her chin. It was rough, the way it always was since they were married, and that confused her.

She'd thought he'd calm down after a while, take his time with her, love her gentle and easy like he had that first time, like she wanted him to, but he hadn't slowed down. It was almost like he hated himself for wanting her and he punished her for it. Although, the pleasure she got out of his rough handling made up for it, in the end.

She had to fight off her urge to claw her way up to his body, to climb onto him and make him fuck her, as his kiss went deeper, became even hungrier. He nudged her back, pressed her into the wall, and spread her knees apart with a firm hand. His fingers found her center, damp from more than the shower, and began to tease her into an anguished moan. He knew how to touch her, how to set her off, to make her come quickly now, and he worked at her in tight circles that tormented her but blew her mind. His other hand came up, to tease at a stiff nipple before his mouth broke away from hers. She would have protested, but she knew where he was headed. His hot mouth engulfed the other tight peak just as her body convulsed against the wall.

He gave a pleased moan against her nipple and was inside of her, her legs wrapped around his waist before she'd even completely finished. The sensation of his thick cock opening her wide, stroking every nerve cell on its way, made her bite her bottom lip to stop another moan. The way he touched her, the way he kissed her, the way he fucked her, all of it said she was his, and he was hers, and it made her clench so hard around him he gave a grunt of surprise.

Hot water sprayed in her face made it hard to breathe, but she didn't care if she suffocated, so long as he continued to fuck her there against that wall. He was over her, inside of her, and she came all over again, unable to escape the emotions, the pleasure he sucked out of her.

When he was finished with his teasing of her, he ducked his head down onto the top of her wet head and held her tightly in place. Careful, precise thrusts, timed to his own perfect cadence, built her right back up again, but this time when she exploded, so did Matteo. They clutched at each other, her nails in his shoulders, his in the globes of her ass, as they cried out together one final time.

He held her until he found his way back to breathing properly and then let her slide down the wall. He looked down at her for a minute, an unguarded minute, where she saw his confusion. She didn't understand, but didn't dare reach out to him, didn't dare move unless he broke the moment. She didn't want him to rush away but knew he would if she moved or spoke a word.

"You, you make me…," he turned away from her and she knew the moment was gone. "Fuck…"

He left her to finish her shower and Marie wondered who had broken him so damn much. Was it Celeste or his mother? Or a past lover? Maybe that's who had turned him into this cold man that couldn't even admit he cared about her, much less loved her. She'd seen it in his eyes, for only a second, but it had been there. Love. Love that confused him, love that made him walk away from her.

She finished her shower and turned the water off. She toweled off slowly, not eager to climb into bed with him just yet. She ran the towel over her hair, squeezed it out until it was only slightly damp. She brushed the strands out and then put on a nightgown before she sat down on the toilet. She didn't want to go in there with him.

A tear slid down from her eye, a tear of hurt and confusion. Everything had been so good between them before her mother died. Everything was sweet, romantic, even the way he'd held off from taking her to bed had been romantic. He'd seemed capable of love, even if he was still a little reserved. This man was almost… broken.

He didn't know how to love, and she wondered if playing the role of the adoring suitor had come easy because he'd been acting. Now, he was a real husband and had no idea what that meant. His father was gone, from what she understood, and he'd been raised by Celeste. He had no real-life examples of what a husband was, except for maybe friends and other family members he might have seen. Did they act like this with their wives? Was it just a Mafia thing to be such a... dick?

She hated to think of him like that, but the way he'd come in here, fucked her, then left her, was kind of dickish. It wasn't like she had a choice in the matter, though. She had no education, no job to support herself, and no hope of ever having the kind of comfort he could give her, at least monetarily. But was money worth being treated like this?

It wasn't the sex that bothered her, she decided, she quite enjoyed that part. It was the way he'd just walk away from her when it was done. It was the fact that he didn't hold her just for comfort anymore, talk to her, or tell her his secrets, that really bothered her. She wanted the intimacy that came from more than just sex, but he wasn't willing to give it to her. Not yet.

Maybe this trust thing was a two-way street. Maybe, if she wanted this to work, she'd have to make an effort to show him that she could be trusted? That she could be a comfort to him in more ways than one?

Earlier she'd thought about how she should be the one in control. And maybe she should be, but first, she'd have to earn his trust. Then, she could learn from him. Learn and make notes, plot a way to make this all work in both their favors.

She didn't hate him, she never had, even when he'd revealed the truth to her. She'd been hurt by him, yes, very deeply, but it wasn't a wound that would never heal. Someone had hurt him, though, the way her momma had tried to hurt her. For years Ruby had tried to make her daughter feel like a mongrel, some unloved and unwanted dog. Those efforts had only made Marie hungry for love, not unwilling to take it.

She wasn't sure she was worthy to be the queen of anything, except someone's heart, her mother had got to her that much. Sometimes, she felt afraid, cowed by the world outside, but she never felt like that with Matteo. She'd always felt… safe, with him near. Even when he had that hard look in his eyes, just before he told her to bend over or open up for him.

She might not be educated, she decided, but she knew an injured animal when she saw one. She knew when someone was afraid of being hurt, knew it well, and Matteo was worse off than she was. What had happened to him?

The need to know became uppermost in her mind, but she wouldn't ask him. She had no idea how she'd find out, but she'd find a way, somehow. She was determined to, for him, for them both. She got up from the toilet and walked into the bedroom they shared when they slept. He was in bed, already asleep.

He turned to her in his sleep and she felt his cock, hard and ready all over again. Even in his sleep, he wanted her. With a naughty smile on her face, she slid her hand down his abdomen, down to that hot flesh that she craved so very much. At first, she simply placed her palm over him, absorbed the sensation of holding him there, of knowing that he was thinking about her, even in his sleep.

She felt a pulse go through him and her hand tightened around him through the flannel pants he had on. She heard a soft moan and looked over at him. His eyes were closed, his breath even, he was probably still asleep. She'd never done this before, touched him so intimately while he was asleep and it felt… good.

He wasn't the guarded man that only allowed her to see what he wanted her to see. He wasn't the man in control. He was simply a man that enjoyed her touch. Unguarded and soft, well, most of him, she thought with a silent laugh. She knew she should probably stop and let him sleep, and a moment of indecision made her bite at her lip before she decided to find out what would happen.

Would he stay asleep, or would he wake up if she continued?

With a careful movement, she slid her hand down his pants to grasp at his naked flesh. His skin was soft and silky as she remembered, yet there was strength beneath that softness, the hardness that could be used to give so much pleasure to them both. Her body reacted to the things she did, which surprised her.

She knew the signs of his arousal could provoke a response in her own body but this was different. She was the one in control, she was the one that decided right now, and that was heady stuff. If she wanted to, she could stop and leave him with an unsatisfied ache, but that's not what she wanted.

What she really wanted was to see him lose control, to let her have it for once, as she gave him some of what he gave her. She stroked him now, slow at first, as she watched his face in the darkness. His breathing didn't change but his face did. His jaw opened slightly and his face became even more relaxed. When she began to stroke him faster, with a tighter grip, he rolled from his side to his back.

Surprised, she paused, waited for his breathing to even out, afraid he'd wake up and take over. She didn't mind another round of sex, her body was hungry for it, but her mind needed this moment. Her mind wanted to know that she could be the one in control, even if it was only this once.

The sound of his breath changed, became gentle and relaxed again, so she moved her hand once more. Slow again, her fingers gripped gently at the base of his cock before she'd stroke up. She judged how fast she should go, how she should grip him, by the sounds he made, and when his hips began to move in time with her hand, she knew she'd found the right pace.

She wasn't exactly sure he was asleep now, but she didn't care. The way his hips danced in time with her hand was too fascinating, the way he moaned softly, over and over again, made her want to climb over him and slide down onto his hard cock, but she held herself back. She pushed his pants down so that she could move her hand more freely so that she could watch what happened when he pulsed out his pleasure.

He was hard, thick, and so ready. She looked at his cock in the soft moonlight and wanted to taste him, wanted to feel that skin against her lips, but held back. She was almost certain he was awake now, but it didn't matter, she was still the one in control. His hands clenched in the sheets beneath him as a groan filled the air and his hips jutted up forcefully into her hand.

Her lips were painfully dry, and she licked them without a thought, too wrapped up in what she was doing to notice. Her nipples were hard, her clit throbbed, and her insides were on fire, but none of that mattered. All that mattered was watching Matteo as he came in her hand.

His cock went really hard and she held her breath in excitement. That's when he pulsed again, only this time, he groaned her name as his cock came to life and spilled the seed he normally spilled inside of her. Over and over he said her name with so much need that she had to squeeze her thighs together to ease the ache there.

Matteo's body relaxed as he finished, a soft sigh of happiness the only sign that he was content. She looked at his seed, all over her hand where she'd caught it. This was what made babies, this was a man's essence. She let him go, rolled out of the bed, and went into the bathroom to wash her hands.

He must have been awake, he'd said her name, so he must have, and that made it even better, she decided as she dried her hands. It meant he'd let her have control, he'd let her take what she wanted. That was all she'd wanted.

10

Matteo drove out to the local boat launch and waited for another car to arrive. The sun had barely risen, the glow of sunrise gleamed only along the tips of the trees out in the spillway. It was cool, almost Christmas, and he had one more meeting to get through before they headed back up to New York to celebrate the holiday.

A black car pulled up, black paint gleaming with black-tinted windows rolled up tight. The car stopped next to Matteo's and a window slid down. The passenger side. A county official sat in that seat and he looked around before he handed Matteo a black folder.

"That everything I need to operate?" Matteo asked softly, his eyes on the folder as he placed it on his seat. He picked up a small messenger bag, the weight of it quite hefty, before he put it in his lap.

"You'll be celebrating a grand opening in February, just as you planned, Mr. Mazza," the older man said from his seat in the other car. The man was pale, pink around the cheeks and the nose, with broken blood vessels along the edges of his nose the only sign that the man had a drinking problem. A problem that Matteo had found out about with the help of a private investigator.

"Thank you, Mr. Smith. Nice doing business with you." Matteo handed over the messenger bag and started the car. The window of the other car went up as Matteo drove away, but he didn't look back long enough to see. He had what he wanted, now he could get on with the rest of his day.

He now had all the licenses and paperwork he'd need to open his casino, the ice cream parlor, and anything else he might happen to want to open, thanks to Mr. Smith's love of bourbon and hookers.

Not that anyone would be surprised that a married man in politics took up with hookers, not really, but the damage would be done to his career if it came out. Matteo had used that information to speed things along when it looked like he was about to hit a wall with local agencies.

His smile widened as he drove down the road. He wondered if Marie would still be asleep when he made it back to the house. He wouldn't mind giving her a little taste of her own medicine. That little tease she'd pulled off last night still had his balls aching this morning, and he knew he'd have to fuck her again before the day was over with.

It would be exquisitely sweet to slide into her, half asleep and still dreamy with warm dreams in her head. The fantasy made him hard as he drove up to the house. He stared up at the white mansion, his eyes on their bedroom window. He turned the car off and went into the house with his ears perked. The tinkle of silverware against a plate told him she was up and having breakfast.

He went down to the dining room and closed the door behind him. With a furtive movement, he locked the door and leaned against it. "Good morning, my dear."

His smile was barely perceptible, a shadow along his lips as he stared at her. She was dressed in a white robe, her thin nightgown hidden beneath. Sunlight started to break in through the windows as she looked up at him, confused, but happy to see him.

"Good morning, Matteo." The furtive smile that played along her lips was tinged with a moment of guilt that she breathed away. "Did you sleep well?"

"I did and went out early to get some business out of the way. Have you finished your breakfast?" He could see she had and was just reading the news on her tablet now. She turned to face him properly, intrigued.

"I have. Are you hungry? I can…" But he interrupted her.

"It's alright. Come here, please, Marie." His brown eyes narrowed as she obeyed, pleased that she was so eager to respond to him. "You were a busy little wife last night, weren't you?"

"Was I?" Her voice went deeper, huskier, desire mixed with worry. Was he upset, she wondered. He knew it by the way she glanced at him and then looked down at the floor as she came up to stand in front of him.

"You were, indeed." His fingers came out as he reached

his right hand out to tug at the belt on her robe. Her dark nipples were prominent against the thin white material of her gown, tight and ready for his touch already. "I thought if you were that eager then you should have a lesson this morning."

"A lesson, Matteo?" Her dark brown eyes, so soft and gentle, came up to meet his with a question. "What kind of lesson?"

For a moment he saw something like defiance there and that pleased him. He wanted her to be the soft, compliant woman he'd met, but she'd have to grow a backbone too. It was something he didn't want to contemplate. He wanted her to be his toy, but she'd have to interact with his family, with the business, and that meant she'd have to toughen up. He didn't want to see it happen, but it was inevitable.

"Yes, a lesson, Marie. Kneel for me, please." She hesitated, her eyes on his lips as if too fascinated to move. "Now, please."

She bent down onto her knees and sat with her bottom along the length of her legs. "Alright?"

"Lean up, so that you can reach my belt." His fingers came out again as she sat up, to run along her jaw, to tilt her face up to him. "Yes, like that."

Her eyes blazed with fire now, orange mixed with the brown to give them a fiery look. The fire of curiosity, the fire of desire. Her desire for him. That only made him harder.

"Open my pants, Marie, take me out." He breathed the words out, softly, so that anyone that might pass by the door wouldn't hear. They weren't alone in the house now.

Her hand came out, flattened over the thick ridge of his cock in his pants. The pressure of her fingers on his dick, those long, delicate fingers that had jerked him off so well only hours before, made a moan form in his throat. He swallowed it down audibly as his nostrils flared.

He felt his eyes narrow as she began to follow his instructions. He wanted to make sure all he saw was her, her reaction to him. He needed to know she wanted him as much as he wanted her. Women could fuck for money, they could fuck for security, but to fuck for the sake of desire, because she wanted to, now that was what got him off. He hadn't known how much he enjoyed that aspect of sex, the woman's response, until he'd got Marie off that first time.

She unzipped his pants after she pulled his belt free, and then, slowly, pulled down his zipper. His pants were weighted down with his phone and wallet so they slid down his legs instantly. He had on black boxers beneath and she slid those down his legs. He stepped out of all of it and unbuttoned his shirt while she slid her hands up his legs and along his flat abdomen, everywhere but the one place he wanted her to touch him.

He'd never been embarrassed about his genitals and didn't feel any shame now as her eyes went wide before they narrowed once again. She was pleased, good.

He was about to fling the shirt away when she grasped at his testicles, gently, as if she knew they were delicate. He didn't know what she knew about sex or a man's body but assumed she was innocent of most things. He let her follow her own path for now, though this was meant to be a lesson. She hadn't hurt him and wanted only to explore him at the moment. There was nothing wrong with that.

Her fingers followed along the edges of the powerful muscles of his thighs again, around the back to grasp at his rock-hard ass. He thrust his hips at her playfully, just enough to show her that his dick, that part of him that jutted out towards her so eagerly, was the part that really mattered. She ran a nail down the round curve of his ass and down the back of his thigh.

Something about it took his breath away. It wasn't that she was taking control, it was that she was exploring, testing out how sensations made him relax. His pleasure mattered to her, and that was… hot.

"What do you want me to do, Matteo?" she asked as she put her hands back into her lap and looked up at him. Her lips were slightly parted, and he could see the edge of her tongue. That's what he wanted, that slick, tiny tongue of hers sucking at his dick, licking him, but he wanted her to explore him at the same time.

"Whatever you want to do, for now, Marie." He leaned back against the door, relaxed into it, as her tongue darted out to wet her lips.

She pulled her bottom lip in, bit down at it gently. It was something every woman did, but when she did it, it made his heart skip a beat with excitement.

He hissed in a breath of anticipation when she reached for him with her right hand, tentative, but sure too. She'd had some late-night practice to learn how he liked to be touched, hadn't she? She thought he'd been asleep, but he'd been awake for… most of it. The part that mattered. He could still remember the way she breathed against his head, the way it came quickly as her arousal grew with his.

Now, he waited, fascinated as she stroked him, her eyes watchful. He didn't push her, but he was going to come in her hands again if she didn't take him into her mouth soon. At this rate, though, he might come the minute she wrapped her lips around his dick. "Fuck."

It came out as a groan that he couldn't stop. He had to get control back before he slipped over the edge too fast. He dug his heels into the floor and clenched his fists against the door. He looked away from her, his jaw hard and his teeth clenched

She responded by leaning into him, her full lips parted, ready with just the tip of her tongue on show. He couldn't help it, he had to look, had to watch as she moved over him. He had to watch this first time she took him between those lips of hers, had to watch her swallow him. It was a battle not to thrust his hips into her face, not to just take what he wanted, hold her still as he fucked her face, but he held himself back, somehow.

He almost blew when her hot, wet lips pressed into the head of his cock, tentatively. She licked him, and that nearly undid him all over again. He would need a dental appointment when this was done, he was going to grind his teeth into dust, he just knew it. But he held it together as she took the base of him in her hand and then moved... down. She only got about halfway down before he hit the back of her throat.

"Swallow, Marie. Pretend you're swallowing me," he urged her, his hands now on her hair, but it was to hold her head and to guide her slowly. His fingers clutched into the silky strands with gentle care, even though he wanted to tangle his fingers instead, wanted to force his way deeper. He couldn't though, not with her. She was too precious for that.

She hummed against him, tried to swallow but couldn't. She'd get the hang of it, eventually. For now, he moved his hand over hers to show her how to touch him. She found a way to please him then, with her mouth and her hand, both used in time together, to take him down into a world of slick silky sex. He forgot to breathe, forgot what it was like to know his own name, as she sucked, licked, stroked him into a new kind of heaven - a heaven she made only for him.

He'd promise her the world, anything she wanted, by the time he found himself too weak to hold back anymore. He'd tried, he'd tried so hard, but he couldn't help himself when she sucked the tip of his cock like she'd never tasted something that fucking good and wanted every drop of it. He exploded into her mouth without warning, and she drank down every drop of him without complaint. He rocked into her mouth, over and over, lost to her.

He needed her as he'd never needed anyone else before in his life. He could admit that to himself. He needed Marie like he needed air, which was one of the reasons he wanted to own her. If she was his, then nobody could steal her away from him. He could please her, make sure she never wanted anyone but him, as long as she was his.

He sank down against the door, his eyes on hers. She still knelt on the floor, her eyes bright with arousal, with her need for him. His clothes were strewn on the floor, his shoes somewhere, and all he had on was an unbuttoned shirt. He was completely debauched, but there she sat, as pure and clean as she'd been the first moment he fucked her.

Later, he'd leave her in a sweaty mess of her own juices, but for now, he wanted only to hold her. She didn't ask questions, she didn't press him for reassurances, she just went into his arms and sank into his body the way he needed her to do. She was his, and they both knew it. That was all that mattered for now. All that he could give her. For now.

11

*S*o many firsts, Marie thought, as she stepped into the limousine at the airport. Her first Christmas away from home, her first ride in a limousine, and her first flight. They'd flown directly from New Orleans to New York on a private jet, also a first. She still had a first, then, for the future. A commercial flight would have taken too long, Matteo had told her, so she still had something to look forward to, eventually.

She tried not to gape out of the window at the sights as they drove away from the airport and into the city. Matteo had an apartment… somewhere. She had no idea what was what in this huge city. New Orleans sprawled along with narrow streets and traffic lights on the side of the road, rather than hanging overhead as they did here.

There was more noise here, more people, more everything. It was almost… frightening. Matteo had warned her: this was a noisy place that was always in motion. At the time, she hadn't thought anyplace could be noisier than

Baton Rouge or New Orleans, but she'd never been to New York. Well, now she had, and it was a little more than overwhelming.

He took her hand as they pulled up to a brick apartment building and a doorman stepped out to open their doors. Yeah, it was that kind of place. She took a deep breath before she stepped out of the car and waited for Matteo to join her. He came around the car while the doorman took out their bags and stacked them on a trolley.

"You alright?" he asked and placed his left palm against the small of her back.

That touch grounded her, brought her back from the edge of panic she'd been headed towards. She smiled at him with reassurance and nodded. "I'm good."

"Good. Follow me, Mrs. Mazza." His voice was low as he spoke, amused. He walked her into the building and to an elevator. A punch of a finger and the very top button lit up.

All that way up, she thought with a glance at him. His face was impassive as if he had no thoughts in his head at all. She knew he must be worried that she might embarrass him in some way, but she was trying very hard to take all of this in her stride. She'd known luxury existed, known that there were people in this world who had no worries about money. She didn't believe, not for one minute, that she'd ever get to have such a moment of such peace.

As the bell dinged and he ushered her out of the elevator, Marie looked around. She had on a pair of black leggings, a long black sweater that came down to her knees, and a pair of leather boots that came up to those same knees; the labels inside each one a suitable label for a place with so much opulence.

It was tastefully done in glass, white objects, and furniture of white leather. Earth tones warmed it up with a brown throw pillow here, a tan one there, a rusty red cover, and a few copper vases on each side of the television screen that was bigger than any TV she'd ever seen. And this was just the living room.

"In here is the bedroom, there's another one at the end of the hall down there. The bathroom is in the middle and the kitchen is off to the left at the end of the hall." He took his black wool coat off and hung it on a peg, along with the stone-gray scarf he'd worn.

She followed his lead and took off her own black coat and hung it up on another peg that lined the wall. She took a deep breath and looked around. The wall of windows drew her and she sat down on the white leather divan that sat before the glass wall invitingly. The city was in the distance, a sprawling wonder of steel, glass, and bricks. A month ago, she'd sat in her own kitchen, a kitchen that was out of date and destined to be sold.

Now, here she was, in New York, in a luxury apartment, as the rain began to fall out of the gray sky that had plagued them since they'd landed. It looked cold, lonely, maybe even unkind. It was a city that didn't care whether you lived or died, and it didn't care who knew it. Marie frowned and wished she was back home, even in the mansion, at least that was familiar, a place that had welcomed her.

"It's not so bad once you get used to it, Marie." He came to sit down beside her and took her hand in his.

"It seems so uncaring, so big." She didn't know how to explain how small she felt as she stared out of those windowpanes. It was an entire wall of them, six by six-inch squares sealed with lead, each one in a larger square. It must be a pain in the ass to keep clean, she thought, and then laughed.

"What's amused you?" He looked over at her and brushed her hair away from her face.

"I was just thinking what a pain that glass must be to keep clean, but it's not my job to keep them clean is it?" She looked back at him, a smile still in place. "I guess we have a cleaner here too?"

"Oh yes, no wife of mine will ever have to clean her own home. We have an image to uphold here, Marie. My family, our business, it's ours, and we don't talk about it in public, ever."

She looked out at the city on display before her and saw lights start to come on as the gray haze turned to darkness. Now, the city came to life. It displayed itself, asked people to come inside to play where it was warm, where you could be whatever you wanted to be.

An urge took over, an urge to kiss him in front of the windows, to show the world who they were together, to show New York, so she did. She leaned into him, took his face in her hands as she climbed into his lap. He allowed her to do as she pleased and kissed her back. For a while.

It didn't take long before her fingers were buried in his hair, her hips strained against him, and her arms were wrapped tightly around his neck. She lost herself in him, and it became apparent that he was just as lost as she was when he groaned and moved. His strong hands held her to him as he pushed her back, sprawled along her body on the long divan.

"Marie, my beautiful, surprising little angel, you turn into such a naughty minx when we're alone." His lips played along her jaw and she turned her head so that he could follow the path down her neck. She could see out and knew anyone could see in if they were up high enough to see into the room. That thrilled her, somewhere deep inside that she'd never known about before.

"You can be whatever you want to be when we're alone. You can do whatever you want…" His lips danced back up to the spot beneath her ear. "But when we leave this place you are my wife, do you understand?"

His hand moved down, to push her sweater up and slide down into the sweet heat between her legs. He went right for the spot that would make her do whatever he asked of her. "Do you understand me, Marie?"

She moaned the only answer she could form as pleasure took over her brain. His fingers stroked at her so perfectly, so expertly that she almost forgot to breathe. Her head tilted back, exposed her throat, and he licked his way down the skin there. She wanted him to go further down, to feel him against her naked flesh, so she ripped her sweater over her head, then threw her bra away.

Instead of traveling down her body, his mouth recaptured hers in a kiss that stole what little breath she had left. His fingers pressed into her, harder, faster, in just the right way, and she gasped into his mouth. She was so close, just a little…

"Tell me, Marie." He broke the spell, leaving her befuddled as he pulled away.

"Tell you what?" she asked, confused. He'd pulled away, left her on the edge of getting off. It almost hurt. She reached for him, desperate to have him back, to have that feeling back.

"Tell me that you will be my perfect little wife when we're not home." His fingers dragged her boots, then her pants and panties away. She was completely naked now, bare to any eyes that could look into the apartment. Her eyes flicked out to see if there were any buildings near enough, but he caught her attention with a finger on the inside of her left thigh. "Marie?"

Brown eyes met brown and she pulled her eyebrows down. Why did she have to agree to that? She opened her legs, a clear invitation to go further. She refused to say anything now, out of nothing more than stubbornness. His eyes narrowed on her, and he moved, knelt over her, and moved down. His lips purred softly against her folds, breathed hot air that made the slick skin burn with cold.

His hands moved to tease at her nipples, then down to tilt her up to meet his face. He didn't do anything else, though, nothing more than breathe against her as his lips touched her bare skin. She tried to press herself up into his mouth, but his hands went tight, his thumbs dug into her hips so she stopped.

Defiance burned from her gaze as she looked down at him, stared into eyes equally defiant. He grinned at her, an evil grin of conquest that nearly had her groaning before his tongue came out and… licked. Her nails dug into the leather of the divan and her knees fell to the side as he licked her again. Slowly, so maddeningly slow, but over and over, until her hips moved again, despite the slight pain of his thumbs against them, because of that slight pain.

When she was near to splitting apart, when she was gasping his name and begging him for more, he stopped. Again.

"Tell me, Marie." He sat up, pulled her close to his hips, his rock-hard cock between them "Tell me you'll do as I say."

She knew he'd never hurt her, he'd never abuse her in any way, but he had ways to make her behave. She could get up, go finish herself off in the shower, but it wouldn't compare to what she felt when he made her come, and he knew it.

There were plans she'd started to form, maybe not a plan to take over the family business completely, but certainly plans to take a place within that business. She wanted to be a part of every aspect of his life. She'd have to give to get, she thought, as she looked up at him.

"I will, Matteo. I'll do whatever you want me to do. Just please, make me come." She reached her hand out to him and smiled.

He moved her hand, guided it to that spot he knew so well, and left it there. He slid his cock along her folds with his now free hand and teased her further. He waited for so long she thought he'd lost his mind, but then, with a grin of satisfaction, he pulled her hips down so that he could fill her.

Marie clasped her legs around him and began to move. She didn't care what he wanted, what his plans were, she needed to come. Her fingers circled her clit as he moved, pulled her up so that her breasts were right there in his face. His lips drew her right nipple into his mouth, tight, snug while his tongue danced over the tip and her world turned inside out. She was certain she'd die, that her heart couldn't take this much pleasure, as waves crested over her, waves of unbelievable bliss.

It wasn't slow and wondrous, it was sudden, over-whelming, and all-consuming. She thought she whimpered his name but wasn't certain. She didn't care, not when the only thing she could think was… nothing. Her mind was in a state of calm and ecstasy. He began to pulse inside of her, her name a moan of his voice against her ear as she leaned down into him with her body boneless and basked in a glow of pleasure.

He held her as they came back to reality, held her close to his slick body. They'd both started to sweat, and she smiled. It enhanced his scent, made his own pheromones stronger, made his cologne warmer, and she inhaled the combined smell that made Matteo so delicious to smell. She licked at his neck to gather that smell into a taste. She savored it as he pulled away and smiled down at her.

"Ready for a shower and some dinner?"

"I'm ready for… more." Her eyes, once so sweet and innocent, were now full of dirty need and delicious desire.

"You have no idea how beautiful you are, do you?" he

spoke softly again as if he didn't really mean to say anything at all.

"I'm not dog-ugly, I know that. But I'm nothing like you, Matteo. I'm not classy, or gorgeous, I'm just me." She let her hair fall over her face and stood up to leave the room.

"No, you are those things, Marie, and so much more." He caught her hand and pulled her back to look at him. "You are perfect, and my wife. I couldn't… I don't want anyone else but you to be that person to me. Do you understand?"

Her heart knocked around in her chest. This was as close as they'd ever come to talking about emotions, even after all this time. His eyes, always so guarded, were open now, full of a plea that she'd never seen there before. He needed reassurance. She'd have never thought that possible. With a gulp of shock and a deep breath, she smiled down at him and squeezed his hand. "I think so. And I won't let you down, Matteo. Not if I can help it. I promise that."

"I know you won't, Marie. Thank you."

He let her hand go and she left him to head to the bathroom. Something had just happened that had been one of those moments that she wouldn't forget. He'd admitted that he needed her, that he cared about her. That was earth-shattering and the smile on her face that wouldn't go away proved it.

$\mathcal{A}$ few days later they were in the back of another limo, on the way to a Christmas party one of Matteo's associates was hosting. Marie was nothing short of stunning in a tasteful but sensual red silk dress, hidden underneath a long leather coat. She wore black heels that made him think all kinds of naughty thoughts, especially with her leg crossed over her knee like that. He was transfixed and didn't notice when his phone began to buzz in the pocket of his suit jacket.

"What?" he asked when he finally felt the vibration and accepted the call.

"We need you down here at the warehouse, boss. We got a problem." The voice on the other end of the line was accented with that thick Bronx sound that he'd noticed made Marie cringe. She preferred the southern drawl, and he had to admit, he did since he'd met her.

"Be there in ten." If Petey was calling him, it was for

something big. Petey didn't call him otherwise. Matteo instructed the driver of the new address to head to and patted Marie's hand when she glanced over at him in question.

"Just some business, baby. Don't worry." He didn't give her details, she didn't need to know, even if he knew exactly what was going on. She was so gentle, naïve about so much, and he wanted to keep her that way if he could. She was an Alfonsi, though, he knew that. It had been playing on his mind since they'd come to New York, back to the home grounds of her father.

The car soon pulled into a warehouse that was dark and empty of anything except some old forging molds that couldn't be moved. It was a front anyway, a place to store products when they needed to. The lights of the car illuminated a trio of men, with another man laid across two wooden boxes off to the side. Matteo tried to hide the man's face from Marie's view as he stepped out of the car but he wasn't sure if he'd managed it or not.

"What's this?" he asked as he looked down at the man.

"Johnny, boss. That little pissant operation that's started up over on Maple Avenue caught him out on a run," Petey, a big man with black hair, black eyes, and a flat nose said to Matteo as he came up to stand in front of Petey.

"Let me see him." Matteo walked over to the man, checked him over, and nodded. "Call Doctor Smith, get him down here to check him over."

Matteo doubted the man would make it as far as a hospital, but maybe the doctor would have something to ease his pain until the end came. He was coughing up blood and his spleen was the size of a watermelon. He wasn't going to make it, Matteo didn't need a medical degree to know that. Something would have to be done about this little upstart gang over on Maple, and it would have to be done quickly. They obviously had no idea who they'd messed with.

"Why did this happen, Petey?" he asked softly, his gaze on the blood that still oozed from the man's lips.

"Johnny's car broke down, we think. We found it a few days ago, but Johnny was nowhere to be found. Maybe they thought he was cutting in on their turf, scoping them out maybe. I dunno, boss. They just beat him with lead pipes, then dragged him over to our side of town like this. They had him for a few days so he might have told them who he was, what organization he works for, we don't know. He probably did and that's why they just dumped him like that." Petey's voice was angry, as angry as Matteo felt. They hadn't even left a message. He assumed they thought this was message enough. Clueless fucks.

"Take a team out there, Petey, once the doctor's done, and inform them of their new station in life." Matteo squeezed his fingers in his palm, angry to lose a man to a gang that barely existed. "Actually, make sure that they never become a problem for us again."

"Sure, boss, consider it done." Petey nodded, a light of anger in his eyes. Johnny was new, but he was one of theirs.

"Call me if you need anything else." Matteo went back to the dying man and saw that the doctor wasn't necessary at all. The shallow breaths and the fading pulse would stop soon.

This was the reality of their lives, the truth hidden in Hollywood's version of Mafia life. Sometimes people died for no good reason. Sometimes they didn't go down in a blaze of glory, or in the arms of some don that treated them like their own child. Nope, sometimes, you died comfortless on two wooden boxes, drowning in your own blood. Not glamorous or romantic at all.

He glanced at the car and hoped Marie couldn't see. He didn't want her night to be ruined. He wanted her to have a chance to dance, to laugh, and to smile as the night wore on, not witness a man's bloody death. "Safe travels, Johnny."

He said the words quietly and then turned away to get back into the car. He tapped the driver's seat ahead of him, and the car pulled away. As they pulled out of the warehouse the glass went up between the back and the driver's portion of the car.

"That's going to be taken care of, isn't it? We're not going to let that go unanswered are we?" Marie asked him from the other side of the car.

His head swung over to her, surprised. "Pardon?"

"That man, someone beat him up on purpose, right? He's going to die? We aren't going to let that stand, are we?" She looked back at him, something hard that glittered in her eyes that surprised him even further.

Maybe she really was an Alfonsi after all. And maybe that wasn't such a bad thing. "It'll be taken care of, don't worry."

He took her hand, kissed her knuckles, and went quiet.

They arrived at one of the classier hotels in the city, a place that was known around the world, and headed into the bar to get drinks.

"I thought we were going to a party for one of your associates?" she asked as they waited for their drinks. "Why isn't it at his house?"

"Too many people to invite. He always has it here." Matteo took a sip of the whiskey that was brought to him and watched her sip at her wine.

"I see." She looked around, her makeup perfect and her body outlined perfectly in that wonderful dress.

He'd already caught more than one man admiring her, despite the wedding ring on her finger. These sharks didn't care if she was married or not. They thought women were pawns, toys to be used and then discarded. And some of the women expected that, truth be told, but not Marie. She was his.

He led her into a dining room where he introduced her to some of the people he wanted her to know and their host before he took her to the dance floor. She wasn't much of a dancer, she'd admitted that long ago, but he'd taught her a few moves that would keep her from being embarrassed. She clung to him as they danced the night away, caught up in each other, to the exclusion of everyone else.

He'd had no idea this was what he'd been missing for so long, but now that he had her, he knew he'd never let her go. Just hearing her laughter as they danced, seeing the way she looked around in wonder, made his heart ache. She'd never had these opportunities, she'd never even been to a party, but now he'd give her as many parties as she wanted if it made her smile like that.

He didn't want his enemies to think him weak, and it was probably a mistake to let the world know that he adored his new wife, but he couldn't help it. For once, Matteo let his guard down. He'd just had a lesson as to why he shouldn't with poor Johnny back there, but he'd also had a lesson in something else - living for the moment.

For once, he was going to do just that and enjoy his time with her.

This was never really a marriage of convenience, he finally admitted to himself. He'd wanted Marie, there was nothing more to it than that. He'd wanted her and he'd taken her before someone else could take her from him.

He twirled her out, only to bring her back into his arms in a spin that made her laugh with giddy joy as her hair flew out behind her. She was a vision of all that was good in the world. Matteo would never use the word good to describe himself. He wouldn't even use the word to describe his family. But Marie was, and yeah, she might be tougher than he thought, she might be made for the job of being a Mafia king's wife, but he knew deep down, there was a gentle side to Marie that he needed.

So long as she was his, he'd protect that. And for the first time, he could admit, that if he wasn't there to protect her, he'd be dead. He would never let her go, not unless staying with him hurt her.

"You're breathtaking, Marie," he said as he pulled her back up to his body to finish the dance.

"You're going to make my head swell up, Matteo," she laughed and put her hand against his cheek for a brief moment. "Thank you."

"I guess you didn't have many compliments, did you?"

"No. Mom made it quite clear that I was far from her favorite person, and she ran off anyone that might be nice to me early on." She headed for a balcony door, overheated now. He could see it in the redness of her cheeks.

He didn't want to interrupt. So often she defended her mother's treatment of her, he wanted to see what else she'd have to say.

"She always told me I was worthless, you know? That no man would ever love me, or even need me. And she said so, so many times that she wished she'd just aborted me..." Her words trailed off and Matteo's fists clenched as he saw the pain in her face, reflected in the glow of street lights and neon signs.

"She was a bitter woman, Marie. I'll spend the rest of my life showing you that if that's what it takes." The words were out before he could stop them. But in a way, he didn't mind, because it was the truth. He would do just that if he had to.

"That's not totally necessary." She gave a short laugh, but it reached her eyes. "My mother was a piece of work - selfish, miserable, and cruel. I've seen enough afternoon talk shows now to know that."

"I'm glad you do, Marie. I wish..." this time he did stop

himself. Wishing was for fools. "Well, I hope we can make a much different future, for both of us."

He didn't tell her about his aunt, still on edge about the woman. He'd have to tell her somehow. But what did he say? Your mother and my aunt could have been twins? You're the product of two of the most selfish people on the planet, and you've walked into a nest of vipers, but I know you're going to change the world for both of us?

There was too much of his own heartache in those words, and he wasn't an emotional kind of man, he reminded himself. With a deep but slightly shaky breath, he led his wife back into the building. He saw so many knowing faces, faces that were full of speculation. A few were buried in phones, no doubt spreading the news to his aunt. He had no doubt he'd get a call before the night was over with.

"You did a good job with the tree, by the way," he said as they went back to the bar. He ordered them two more drinks and then they went to sit alone at a table.

"Thanks. I've never had one so big, or so many decorations. Actually, Mom stopped even getting them when I was around 5. Said they were too messy and cost too much." She sipped at her cold white wine and looked at him. He didn't see self-pity in her gaze, just a truth she wanted to share. "After that, I couldn't afford one, even a fake one, so we did without. Mom didn't care about any of that, especially after she was excommunicated."

Her eyes went round as if she'd gone further than she'd meant.

"Pardon? They still do that?" He hadn't known it still happened.

"Oh yes, well, desecration and profaning the church will get that, don't you know?" Her cheeks went pink so he didn't press her for more information. He could just imagine what the woman had done. He'd learned enough about her now to know, he thought. Something rude, selfish, and with no other goal than attention in mind, no matter how that attention might impact her daughter. Poor Marie.

"Well, it sounds like you need more time in front of that tree of yours, then, Mrs. Mazza." He grinned as he leaned in to whisper into her ear. "Want to head home?"

"I'd like that." She turned just enough to smile into his eyes. "I'd like that a lot, Mr. Mazza."

He called to have the car brought around and in no time at all, they were changed into pajamas and staring up at the lit tree in the dark living room. It was over 10 feet tall and covered in every kind of decoration she could find. There was even thin silvery tinsel hanging off the thing. It was like a kid's dream, and Matteo knew that's exactly what it was, the tree she'd dreamed about since she was a kid denied such frivolous things.

He held her as they drank Irish coffee and watched the lights change on the tree. She even had some old-fashioned ones that looked like candles with bubbles in the long glass light section.

"Thank you," she said with a pleased sigh. "Thank you for giving me this, Matteo."

"It's my pleasure, Marie." A bit too formal, maybe, but

he was new to all of this being a good husband stuff. He didn't want to be an asshole, after all, just in charge.

"I love that thing more than I thought I would. It's amazing really." She leaned back into his chest and sighed. That was all the thanks he needed - her contented sigh. Maybe a brighter future was in store for him, after all. Once he got Celeste out of the way, that is.

13

"I want to learn to play the piano," she said to Matteo the next afternoon. He'd put on some music as they relaxed together after lunch. It was classical music, Chopin he'd told her.

She rested between his thighs, her head on his stomach as she stared at the Christmas tree. The thought had only just occurred to her, she'd always wanted to be able to play an instrument, but there'd never been money for lessons. Her mother wouldn't have allowed her to have lessons, anyway, even if those lessons were free. Marie might enjoy them, and Ruby wouldn't have allowed her unwanted daughter even that small amount of satisfaction.

"You can do whatever you want, Marie. You can take piano lessons, go back to school, become an astronaut, whatever you desire, darling." His voice was low as if he was almost asleep.

She liked these moments, cuddled together, just enjoying being close to one another. Affection had been one of the many things Marie had been starved of her entire life, so these moments were precious to her. "I doubt I could be an astronaut at my age. Maybe piano lessons are something too far out of reach too, but still, I'd like to try."

"Then I'll have it arranged." He ran his fingers into her hair to massage her scalp. "After we get Christmas and the New Year out of the way, I'll have someone come in to teach you."

That meant he'd have to buy a piano. The thought made her smile. Things like that always did make her smile, though. He didn't think anything about it, but to her, it was like her birthday and Christmas rolled into one every time he bought her something she'd done without her entire life, but had always wanted.

It was like the laptop he'd bought for her. He'd noticed she didn't have one, so he bought her one. She needed it, he'd told her, but she wasn't sure why she needed one exactly. She'd taken the present and explored the Internet and what was out there in the world through it.

She'd started a private blog once she found out those kinds of things existed and had been writing in it, like a diary. She was good at typing, which had made her think about the piano lessons again. Would it be the same? Playing the piano, would that take the same finesse? As the music played she thought about it more and almost laughed because she'd soon find out.

"How are you feeling?" he asked, nonchalantly.

Matteo wasn't a very talkative man sometimes, but since they'd come to New York he'd opened up to her more. She knew there were still secrets buried inside of him, but he'd allowed her into his world. Mostly because he needed to know how she was. He wasn't concerned about his own emotions, or what he needed, but with her and her needs.

"I'm fine. A little nervous. We're going to your aunt's for Christmas dinner tomorrow. I'm not sure what to wear, or how to act, I'm really worried I'll embarrass you."

"Ah, my aunt. She's flying back in from Italy tonight. She's been told about us now. She's… calm." Matteo chose his words carefully, but she felt the way his fingers tensed on her scalp before they relaxed again. He wasn't totally pleased about his aunt coming home or being told about them then.

He never talked much about her, but from the things he said, Marie knew he didn't like the woman very much. That didn't make her own situation any easier to deal with. She was the product of her husband's affair. Trying to keep it straight in her own mind could get confusing at times.

How would Celeste treat her, she wondered. Her birth wasn't something that Marie could help, but she knew that she wouldn't be a happy reminder to Celeste, a memento of her husband's infidelity. Marie wouldn't be surprised to be greeted with hatred, especially since Marie had taken it all a step further and married Celeste's nephew. The woman had to be intelligent, which meant she would know that their marriage was a ploy to negate the debt owed by Ruby.

"Do you think she'll hate me?" Marie asked quietly, almost afraid to actually voice it. The question was a stupid one, of course Celeste would hate her.

"I don't know. Celeste is… her own woman. She doesn't reveal much to anyone." Matteo's fingers moved down to the back of Marie's head to knead at the spot where her spine met her skull.

"She took over the family business after my father died," Marie pointed out, but let him interrupt.

"She did. There wasn't anyone else to take his place. Well, there would soon be you…" his words slowed, then stopped.

It had occurred to him finally, then. She didn't smile or tense up. She forced herself to stay relaxed and to enjoy the moment with her husband.

"I'm not ready for leading anything like that. You're the one that's been trained to take over for the woman that is, well, my stepmother. Odd to think that, isn't it?" The term was something she'd considered over the last few weeks, even if it didn't seem right.

"I don't know what she'd be called, technically. I suppose stepmother would be right." She could feel his tension in the strong way his fingers dug into her muscles, but she didn't complain. "She's now your aunt by marriage, as well."

He gave a soft chuckle before releasing a deep sigh.

"We're in a strange situation," she said, just to have something to say. "It's not going to be easy. None of it."

"No, it won't be. It never is, though, not when she's involved."

"Can you help me pick out hairstyles and clothes?" She sat up and turned to look at him, her knees pulled up to her chest. "I want to look… right."

"Let's see what you have in the closet, and then we can see if we need to go shopping." He smiled to reassure her and moved to the edge of the couch. "As for your hair, that kind of bun thing you had it in a few weeks ago will do."

"The French twist? Okay, that's simple enough to do." She'd learned it from a video online, one she'd found on her phone, and had recreated it.

They went into their bedroom and she opened her closet. Dresses, shirts, pants, skirts, blouses, sweaters, and shoes filled the space. She looked at Matteo with a trace of guilt in her eyes. "I might have gone overboard."

"No matter, you deserve it all." He kissed her forehead and pulled out a black dress that went down to her lower calves. "Something in this shape, but not so… black."

"Oh? Okay, well, I have it in emerald green." She pulled it out of the green side of the closet. She'd coordinated it all by colors, which might be OCD she thought, but it made sense to her and that's what mattered.

"Hmm. Maybe not." He frowned and looked along the greens before he moved down to the reds. "This maybe."

He pulled out a long sheath dress, put it back, then pulled out a red lace and silk Valentino dress. The very top of the dress and the sleeves were lace with ruffles that came just above her wrist. It was mid-thigh length, tasteful, sophisticated, and just a little sensual.

"Perfect," he declared. He pointed at a pair of red heels and then went to her jewelry box. He'd filled that lately too until she almost felt as if every day was Christmas. He pulled out a pair of gold and ruby earrings, studs, and a ruby ring that matched.

"That's the decoration taken care of," he said with a smile and turned to look at her. "Now, what else?"

She laughed because it had taken him five minutes, whereas she'd done nothing but think about which dress would be appropriate for days now. The dress he'd chosen was one she'd dismissed as too girlish so she asked him why he'd chosen it.

"Celeste and my family, the friends she's invited to this exclusive dinner, will all judge you on the front you present. A sexy dress will make them think you're a tramp that married me for my money. A formal dress will look like you're trying too hard. This dress is too much for a board meeting, but it's perfect for this kind of dinner. You'll feel confident and look the part."

"It sounds so simple when you put it like that." She looked down at her nails, manicured with gel almond-shaped nails and a nice scarlet red polish with a slight hint of black glitter at the tips. "I feel so inadequate sometimes."

He came up to her and tilted her chin up to look into her face. "You've not had a lifetime to learn things like this, Marie. You had a lifetime of trying to survive, of dealing with a mother that didn't want you, of feeling like your only purpose was to be a servant. Well, that's over with, baby. You're my wife now, and you get to think about the important things, but also silly things like this, that don't really matter, but they do matter to people in this world you've found yourself in."

He pulled her down to the bed, an understanding smile warmed his eyes as he did.

"I couldn't do this without you." She clutched at his

hands, desperate for the comfort only he could give her. "I'd be so lost."

"You wouldn't have to if it wasn't for me." Guilt marred his features, and they both looked away. It was the first time they'd really had any kind of conversation about the matter. She waited, breath held, as he sat there, looking for the right words to say. "What I did, I did for family. I did because I thought it would save us both in the end. It wasn't right, but I can spend a lifetime making it up to you."

"That sounds good to me." She hadn't exactly forgiven him for the lies, the untruths he'd told her. Or the deception he'd been a part of, for that matter. Still, it was hard to stay angry with him, to be cold and unfeeling towards him when he made her feel like a queen every single day. In bed and out of it. "I don't really want to do this. I feel like I'm walking into a viper's nest, but it has to be done, right?"

"Unfortunately, it does. And believe me, I'd rather not go either, but we have to. If I'm going to take over for Celeste, then I have to make an appearance. Besides, a few of my cousins aren't too bad. I think you'll like my cousin Trina, in fact. She's the most playful of all of them."

"A friend would be nice." She hadn't thought any of his family would be the kind of people that would talk to her. She'd assumed every single one of them would turn their noses up at her. And the friends too, apparently there would be friends of the family there as well. "You don't think she'll try to do something to humiliate me, do you?"

She looked at him earnestly, worried that this would be the case.

"More than likely, yes. You'll have to be on your guard, cautious, around all of them. Even Trina until you get to know her. My advice would be to make small talk, stay away from politics, and keep the conversation as light as you can. With Trina, you'll get to know her over time, but still, just in case, be cautious."

"We really have to do this?" she asked again.

"Yes. It'll be like tearing off a Band-Aid. Once it's over, it should get better, easier to do. And I'll be there don't forget. You won't be alone."

"Good." She took a deep breath and tried to calm herself. "I hope I can get to sleep tonight. I'm so nervous about all of this I could barely sleep last night."

"I'll make sure you get to sleep." He gave her a saucy wink and stood up. "Come on, enough of this now. It's Christmas Eve and you have more presents to open."

"More?" She looked at him in surprise, what else could he possibly get her?

"Yes, more," he laughed, pleased that he could do all of this for her obviously.

"Shouldn't we save them for tomorrow evening?" She tried to stall him, a little overwhelmed. She had so many toys and gadgets now she barely knew what to do first most of the time.

"Maybe so. But there's one I want you to open up today. I want to see what you think about it." His voice sounded odd and she looked at his back as they walked back into the living room. What was this present then?

He gave her a small box, about six inches by six inches wrapped in white paper with a red ribbon. There were more presents under the tree, some for him that she'd bought, and she'd thought the rest were for his family. That didn't seem to be the case.

With a befuddled smile she tugged at the ribbon and pulled the paper off. Inside the box, around three inches deep, sat a small pistol, small enough that it would fit in her hand. The silvery metal gleamed and she looked down at the thing with curiosity. Guns didn't frighten her, but she had no idea how to use one.

"What do I do with this?" She looked at him as the reality of the life they would live together hit home, hard. He thought she needed a weapon to defend herself, but from whom? His aunt? People outside of the family? Who exactly was a threat to her?

"Keep it with you, in your bag, or in a holster if you want. But always keep it with you. Remember what happened to your father? That could still happen. My world isn't exactly the most angelic, Marie, I think you know that by now." His accent thickened as he spoke, the clipped tone that only sounded good on him. When other people up here spoke, the accent was an oddity that still made her brain stutter until she caught up. She was used to hearing Matteo speak now but being in a crowd of people that spoke like him was sometimes overwhelming.

"We'll get through this, Marie, don't worry. Life with me isn't going to be simple, it may even get dangerous sometimes, but I will always, *always,* do my best to protect you, I swear it."

She looked down at the gun, then back up at him. "You'd better show me how to use it then."

"What? Don't all you southern girls climb out of the cradle knowing how to handle a gun?" He looked surprised.

"My mom didn't have time to show me a lot of things, and well, you know what happened to my dad." She frowned but then smiled a saucy smile. "It's something else you get to teach me."

Her wink made him laugh happily. That made her smile right back at him. This wouldn't be so bad. She hoped.

14

This was going to be terrible she just knew it. She pulled at the lace at her collarbones to try to loosen it up. The problem wasn't the red lace, though, it was a knot in her chest somewhere, a knot of fear that she was determined nobody would see.

"Take it easy, baby." Matteo's hand guided her up the steps to the brownstone house, and he rang the doorbell. "It's almost over."

"It's only beginning," she reminded him with a mutter.

"True, but that first moment will be over with, and you'll be able to feel your way through this from there. Now smile and fake it with me." He leaned over to peck her on the nose just as the door opened.

"Matteo!" A young woman, roughly around Marie's age, answered the door with a happy shriek. Marie winced a little as the woman flung her arms around Matteo's neck before she pulled away just as quickly. "And you must be Marie. Welcome to the family, I'm Trina."

"Hi," Marie spoke softly and nearly stepped back in surprise, but she stood her ground and lifted her head up. "Thanks for the welcome."

"Come in, let's meet the family, shall we?" Trina pulled them into a foyer and Marie looked around. The room was open, and she could see now that the building had once been three buildings but was now one. Two stairways led up to another floor, and that's where the slim young woman took them. "The first floor is mainly a study, the kitchen, a bathroom, up here is where you'll find everyone. The dining room is off to the left there, and over here is a ballroom as Aunt Celeste likes to call it."

Trina, a pretty woman with dark gray eyes, black hair, and olive skin, pushed open a door to show a crowd of people standing around talking. Along each wall were tables and chairs, and at the front of the room by the door was a bar with some snacks on trays.

Marie took a calming breath and walked into the crowded room, filled with over 30 people, and looked around. Everyone was dressed exquisitely, with jewelry dripping from every finger and earlobe, even the men. Some were old, some younger, none that were under the age of 15 as far as Marie could tell.

"This is my mother, Audrina," Trina said as she came up next to an older woman with silky black hair down to her waist, dressed in a long, dark-green velvet dress. It complemented the bright-red velvet dress that Trina had on. "And this is my dad, Solomon O'Toole."

The man was older, dashing in that gray hair at the temples kind of way, with the gray eyes that matched his daughter's. The couple smiled at Marie and greeted her and Matteo. Marie surmised that Trina's mother must be the blood relative, a man with an Irish last name surely wasn't a brother of Celeste's.

"Welcome to the family," Solomon said somberly, and his wife frowned.

"He makes it sound terrible, we aren't that bad, really." She smiled and leaned over to peck Marie's cheek. Marie wasn't short, but she wasn't too tall either. She matched these two women in height, at least, especially since they all wore similar heels. "Celeste hasn't come down yet."

That part she said softly to Matteo, but Marie heard her.

"And my mother?" Matteo asked, his voice as quiet as Audrina's.

"She's not well, Matteo." Audrina looked away, and Marie knew she was lying, but why would she lie? Why lie about his mother's absence? "She's sorry she couldn't make it."

"No matter." Matteo looked down at Marie and winked. "Another time."

Marie didn't quite understand how a mother could let another woman take her child away, but she wasn't this family or Matteo's mother. She had a feeling Celeste was the type of woman that you didn't often say no to, as well. It was all strange, but no stranger than her own parentage, or upbringing. Just a different kind of strange.

Marie smiled politely as extended relatives were introduced, more cousins, and then a slew of family friends. She forgot most of their names after a while because it all became a blur of introductions, small talk, and then on to the next one. Marie felt anxiety tighten her throat with each passing name, with each new face, but she pushed it down.

She'd learned to hide her emotions from her mother, learned to hide hunger and misery from her teachers and the occasional social worker, she could get through this. She smiled, nodded, spoke when she had to, and held onto Matteo's hand like it was her one and only lifeline.

She'd had two glasses of white wine by the time his aunt made her entrance. The entire room went quiet as the door opened and people saw who was there. They went quiet not only because she was the head of the family, but because she had eyes only for Matteo. Very angry, very cold eyes, Marie noted.

He stood his ground though and didn't let go of Marie's hand at all as the woman in a silver sequined dress that fit her slim form snugly walked up to greet them. Her hair was black as night, streaked with a few strands of silver, but it didn't make her look older, it made her somehow sexier, but in the way that mythical vampires and goddesses of old could be alluring, sensual, but still quite deadly.

"Matteo. I see you've brought your… wife." Her brown eyes took in her nephew with disinterest before they turned to Marie. "Hello."

"Hi," Marie said with a short smile. She looked the woman in the eye, afraid that if she showed deference Celeste would try to walk all over her for the rest of her life, but also afraid that not showing deference could be a deadly mistake. She chose to go with not being a doormat.

"So, you're my dead husband's child. Welcome home." She held her cheek out and Marie bent to peck at it. Celeste pulled away with cold eyes, surprisingly cold eyes for someone with eyes that dark. "I hope you enjoy your time with us."

Celeste said it as if Marie had only come for a vacation and nothing more. Matteo was about to reproach her when Celeste moved away and headed for Trina's mother and father without another word.

"Well, we survived that," Matteo said and Marie breathed a sigh of relief.

"We did. For now. I have a feeling that's not the end of it." Marie clutched at his hand and they left the room. He took her out to a balcony at the back of the building, even though the air was cold. He knew she needed a break from the hot room and the strained nerves the situation was causing her, and she was grateful. "Thanks."

"My pleasure. Believe me. I need a break as much as you do." He leaned against the railing and looked at the small patch of garden behind the building.

"Well, as you said, the hard part is over. We get through dinner, and then we're free for the rest of the night." She sat down on a small chair in the corner of the balcony, cold but happy to be out of that room. He'd been right, she saw the way everyone stared at her, whispered as she moved around the room. They'd accepted her, but only because of Matteo. They would turn on her if it wasn't for him and throw her out to the wolves. Or perhaps they were the wolves.

"We're going straight home. We don't exchange gifts so once dinner is done, we can leave." He sounded as relieved as she felt.

"Merry Christmas, baby," she said to him with just a trace of sarcasm.

"It will be once I get you home, Marie." He took one last deep breath and turned back towards her. "Are you ready to go inside? She'll be ready to start dinner now that she's come down."

"Quite dramatic, isn't she?" she whispered close to him her arm twined around his.

"Very. That entrance was very much planned, believe me." Matteo swore under his breath and looked down at her. "I'm sorry I got you into this."

"It's just family politics, Matteo. Don't worry. I'm not a scared little bunny about to scamper away." She reassured him with a smile, but it was fake. She wanted to run very far away, as fast as possible, and they both knew it.

"You're a brave lady, Marie, even if you don't know it." He pecked the top of her head and they went into the ballroom to find it almost empty. Trina was still in there.

"Come on, let's eat so we can get out of here. I have a real party to get to later and this is cutting into my drinking time." Trina laughed with a sweet trill as she came up to them, a contrast to her words. The words came out edgy, tough, but that laugh was pure sugary sweetness.

She was an enigma that Marie couldn't figure out so she

stopped trying to and went with it. They went into a long room with a very long table inside. People were sat on each side with Celeste at the head. Three places had been saved up at the top by Celeste. Matteo, Marie, and Trina's places she soon figured out as Trina walked up to her aunt and sat down.

"Good to see you again," Celeste started right away, and Marie turned to her with a frozen smile.

"Hello. Thank you for having us over for this special occasion." Marie had practiced that in her head a hundred times, changed the words, tried to perfect the sentence until that was what she came up with.

"It's my pleasure. It's not every day a woman gets to have her husband's illegitimate child at her table, after all. It's a… special treat, isn't it?" Celeste pursed her lips and looked down her nose at Marie with nothing but pure hatred.

"I can go if you prefer?" Marie met that glacial stare head-on without a flinch. "I was under the impression you invited me here, but if not, I can leave with my deepest apologies."

"No, of course not. You're right. My apologies." From the way her jaw worked and her eyes closed, Marie knew Celeste wasn't really sorry at all. It was more like she was trying to control her disgust. Marie couldn't blame her, but then, Celeste did invite her here. It was her own fault she had to eat with her dead husband's bastard, wasn't it?

"Thank you." Marie turned away to look at Matteo, sat across from her on Celeste's right.

"Stab that old biddy with your butter knife, Marie,"

Trina whispered once Celeste's attention had turned to someone two seats down from Matteo.

"What?" Marie gasped softly and turned to stare at Trina with horror.

"I'm joking, just joking. Calm down." Her hand came down over Marie's wrist and she gave her a conspiratorial wink. "Although, she would deserve it after what she just said."

"I couldn't." Marie paused, saw the hopeful, playful look in Trina's eyes, and decided that the woman really was only messing around with her. "The knife is too dull."

Trina laughed that sweet tinkle of a laugh again and winked at Marie. She did a lot of winking this woman, Marie decided. "We're going to get along fine."

"Matteo said we would," Marie responded and pulled back as a woman in a black maid's uniform came up to fill her glass with red wine. Marie pulled up the glass and tilted it at her new friend. She hoped. "To new friends."

"To new lives," Trina added and they both took a sip of their wine before a man in a black suit came out and started to spread food along the table.

Marie ate a few slices of turkey, some cranberry sauce, and a few bites of mashed potatoes before her stomach started to rebel. It wasn't happy about eating right now, not under this much stress, and she looked over at Matteo. He smiled a smile that was only for her across the black marble table.

Marie didn't notice the tableware, it might have been white or black, or it could have been solid gold. All she noticed was how the moments ticked by, and how the urge to run away only increased. Matteo noticed she'd stopped eating and stood up.

"Thank you for your hospitality, Aunt Celeste, but I fear my wife may be a little under the weather. Perhaps it's the same bug my mother has." The twist of his lips told her it wasn't the same "bug", but she wouldn't pry. She'd already heard one couple whispering about his mother's fondness for gin. This was just a dig at Celeste then, the cause of the woman's drinking, or so the whispers had said. "In any case, thank you for the food and your company. I hope to see you again soon. Good night all, merry Christmas."

Before anyone could say anything else, before Celeste could protest at all, Matteo had swooped Marie up and led her out to the foyer to collect their coats. Matteo was all but running by the time they got there, and Marie giggled. They snatched their coats and ran out of the door to the car without even putting the coats on first.

Matteo hit the button to unlock the doors of the car and they hopped in and sped away. "I'll pay for that later, one way or another. But you know what? I don't really give a fuck. I've got you all to myself again."

He kissed her hand in his, then let it go to change gears.

"I hope it was worth it. I could have laughed my heart out at the shock on her face, but I wanted out so desperately that I didn't care if we were rude or not."

"Maybe they'll put it down to young love. Again, I don't care." He laughed, but the mention of love was like a bucket of cold water over them both.

"You don't have to say it, Matteo. I know why we're married. We're friends as well as lovers. Maybe that's better than other kinds of marriages." She brought the sparkle back to his eyes with that, or maybe it was just the streetlights. This, too, didn't matter.

They had each other, and love match or not, they were good together. That was good enough for her, for now.

15

They rushed through the door to the penthouse in a daze of holiday cheer. Marie had made her own stamp on the place over the last few days, with a few dozen holiday scented candles and warming air fresheners that filled the house with the scent of spiced apples and cranberries.

It made her smile even broader as they threw their coats on the pegs on the wall, and she leaned back against the door. "This is absolute heaven, do you know that? When I was a little girl, I'd dream of being able to have a tree similar to this one and to have the house smell so… good."

"I guess things like that were a luxury for you both then?" Matteo went into the living room and poured two glasses of whiskey.

"It was, and when Mom became bedbound, well, the atmosphere wasn't always pleasant there. I don't want to bring the tone down, so let's leave that in the past, alright?"

She pulled away from the door and went into the living room.

She'd already had three glasses of wine that night and she was a little tipsy already. She sipped at the strong liquor and gasped as it took her breath away. It was a nice flavor, though, and she cupped the glass above her breasts as she went to the couch and sat down.

"Matteo?" she asked, her mind turning to that first day when he'd taken her there on the divan in front of that window.

"Yes?"

"Would you, that is, can you…" She felt her cheeks turn red and she looked up at him from beneath her lashes. "Come here?"

"Oh, now, baby, if you want something, you'll have to ask for it…" He caught the hint of her blush and smiled a knowing smile.

"Fine. I have all of those presents over there, but do you know what I really want for Christmas?" Her legs opened at the knees a little and her voice dropped down a little, the way it always did when she was aroused.

"I have an idea." He knelt on the floor in front of her and ran a hand up between her thighs. The heat of his skin against her thighs brought her mind into crystal-clear focus.

"You're going to make me say it, aren't you?" Normally, Matteo was the dominant one, he directed what happened. But every now and then, like now, he'd let her have her way.

"Yes, baby, you have to say it. You don't have to ask me,

or offer me anything, just tell me what it is you want." He leaned back on his legs, took off his suit jacket and tie, and then leaned back into her.

"No," she frowned and waved her hand at him in objection. "I want you totally naked."

The flush traveled lower now, from her cheeks and down to her chest. Arousal flooded through her body, brought it to life, forced her embarrassment out so that all that remained was a woman that knew what she wanted. Her arousal only grew as Matteo stood up and did as instructed. The shirt dropped to the floor, then his shoes flew away, followed by his pants.

He stood in front of her, let her inspect him, and she grinned because she knew he was hers. All of him, from that broad chest to those hard abs, and down, lower, to the part of him that throbbed even now. He was ready for her, but then he always was.

Just as she was always ready for him. She slid down on the couch seat so that her legs sprawled out and she revealed the tops of her nude stockings. There was even a hint of the black lace panties she wore, she saw when she glanced down at herself. "Take off my panties, Matteo."

"Yes, ma'am." That defiant smirk was still full of promise, despite the way he drawled.

His fingers slid up her outer legs until they hooked into her panties. He pulled them down slowly with a kiss for each new inch he revealed. Her breath caught in her chest when the panties finally slid down off of her bottom and his lips found the very top of her bare cleft. His tongue slipped out now, to taste the very edge of sex.

"More." She made a demand now, not a request. "Taste me more, Matteo."

She twisted her hips up into his face when the slick heat of his tongue came out to swipe at her clit more forcefully. Again, he flattened his tongue on her and licked her sensitive flesh, over and over.

Pleasure surged through her, around her, within her as Matteo worked to give her exactly what she asked for. His fingers came up to skim over her folds, to seek within, until he found the entrance he was looking for. She groaned with sheer bliss as she felt him slide two fingers inside of her, deep into her until he couldn't go any further.

Sprawled there on the couch, free of all of her worries, Marie rocked her hips into him, into his mouth, into his fingers, taking the enjoyment he offered her freely. She didn't realize she was moving, rocking closer to him and off the couch until her ass was free in the air. His free hand cupped her ass and drew her to him to steady her as she began to tremble beneath.

"Don't stop, Matteo. Don't stop," she urged him on, desperate as she felt a flutter begin deep inside of her. Just a moment more, and she knew she'd be in heaven. "Don't you dare stop."

It came out as a powerful, guttural growl, something she didn't recognize from herself, but it also pleased her. Her hips twisted and her spine turned until his face was pressed against her and her own face was pressed into a pillow. She didn't care, didn't mind if she couldn't breathe, because the world became nothing but pure bliss as his fingers plunged into her at just the right angle.

"That's it, Matteo. Fuck, that's it!" she screamed the words out as her body took over and she lost all control.

It washed over her again as he continued to tongue her. Even after the waves stopped he carried on, until she couldn't take anymore and came again.

She was wrung out, devoid of all thought when he finally pulled away and turned her over. His hands guided her head down, then pushed her dress up over her ass. With a hard tug of her hips, he plunged into her, ready to empty himself inside of the sweet little vixen that never left his thoughts.

"Mine" was the only word he uttered when he finally found his release within her and it made something go tight inside of her chest, something that spread out as a warm glow of happiness. She loved the way he claimed her, even if she shouldn't.

She knew she was supposed to be a strong, independent woman, and she was in most aspects of her life. But when it came to Matteo, she was only his. That was all she ever wanted to be she realized as she slid down to the thick carpet and curled into him. Just his.

She wouldn't say it, wouldn't make a fool of herself, not if he didn't want to be loved. Or to love her. She suspected he loved her though, but Matteo was the kind of man that wasn't very expressive in many ways. He could be happy, smile, laugh, show anger, even adoration. Now that she'd met his aunt, she could see why he sometimes seemed so… cold.

She pulled him into her arms as he rolled into her. She reached for a remote on the end table and turned on the gas fire that hid behind a panel in the wall. The panel moved aside and the flames came to life as they curled around each other. Matteo reached up to the couch and pulled down a blanket and two pillows, one for each of them.

"We could just live here, in the living room, couldn't we?" he asked as the flames lit the room with warmth. "Never go out into the world again. We could have groceries delivered, and anything else we need, and just live here for the rest of our lives."

"We could." She smiled and glanced up at him. "I'd have to go out every now and then, to see the doctor for my birth control pills."

"Ah, those. We could arrange to have the doctor come here. Don't worry." He patted her bare bottom, obviously pleased with himself. "There's an answer to everything, I just know there is."

"What about the family business?" It wasn't a subject she really wanted to broach but felt it was worth the question.

"Fuck it," he said suddenly and sat up. "It's a pain in the ass and I'm tired of it."

"Are you?" She turned to her side and looked up at him.

"I am, but it's also my responsibility now. Everybody in the family counts on me more and more as Celeste spends more time in Italy. It's somehow my job. I'm not even related to Nick, you know?"

"I do know, yes. But to be blunt, Matteo, I don't think I could run it, and I seriously doubt Celeste would allow me to. So, it's left to you isn't it?"

"Would you want to be more involved? Even knowing that it's dangerous?" He slid back down to join her on the floor once more and stared at her, completely unguarded now.

"I think I would. You'd have to teach me a lot, I guess, but I'm not a stupid woman, and I took care of everything for my mother. I'm capable of learning, even if all I have is a high school education."

"I went to a Catholic high school. All I wanted was to go to a public school and get away from all of those priests and nuns." He shuddered as he rolled to his back and stared up at the ceiling. "You can study online, you know? NYU has a lot of online programs now, we could get you into some classes at the school, too, if you wanted."

"Maybe so." She rolled to face him and felt a new hope start to glow into life. "I could, I guess."

"You aren't too old, you know?" He brushed hair back from her still red face and smiled. "You can do it if you want to."

"I might." Her eyes moved to the Christmas tree, and the pile of presents beneath it. "Do you want to open the presents tonight, or in the morning?"

She'd bought a few things for him, things she hoped he'd like. She was more excited about watching him open his presents than she was about her own. He'd given her so much already, and she had a feeling that the gift giving wasn't over.

"Now, I think. I'm curious to see what you've got for me." He sat up and leaned back against the couch as she crawled, naked, to the tree, and pulled presents over to where they sat.

"I hope you like them." He opened the first one carefully, slowly, as if he'd never been given a gift before and wanted to relish it.

The paper opened to reveal a collection of vinyl records. The Beatles, originals, all of them. "Where on earth did you find these?"

He looked at her amazed.

"In a shop not far from here. They have quite a large collection of them." She glanced at the bigger box and knew that the contents must be apparent now.

He pulled the paper away, eager to find out what was inside. His eyes gleamed when he saw the chrome and red-painted record player inside. Immediately, he got up, plugged the player in, and put on the first record. The sounds of so long ago came to life the instant the needle met the vinyl and they both smiled.

"This might be the best present ever. I have the digital versions of all of these songs, but it never occurred to me to find the records. Thank you, Marie." He leaned over to kiss her and pull her close.

"That's not all of them, but we can wait until tomorrow, if you'd like, to open the rest."

"Aren't you curious about what I got for you?" he asked and put a kiss on her head.

"I am, but it can wait. I'd like to listen to this a little more." She repositioned her head on his chest and began to hum along with the music.

She'd never have guessed, not in a million years, that

she'd be in a New York penthouse on Christmas Day, married to a man who gave her everything she could ever want. She'd spent her days in misery, trying to get through each day as best she could. People rarely spoke to her, and life was one routine after the next. Fix breakfast, clean her mother, clean the house, make lunch, go out to get the shopping, come home and make dinner, go to bed, rinse, repeat, and carry on.

Now, her mother was gone, and though it wasn't a good thing, Marie couldn't be sad about it anymore. The more Matteo had shown her about the world outside of her Louisiana home, the more she realized how much her mother had denied her. She knew her mother had her reasons, that life hadn't exactly been fair to Ruby, but she had added cruelty to her very long list of sins. She'd denied Marie the most basic comforts in life, even before she'd become ill.

Although even after her mother had become ill, she'd been cruel to her only daughter. There was no need for it, but her mother had continued her cruelty. She didn't want to dwell on it, but at that moment couldn't help it. She'd been deceived by Matteo, that was true, but he'd given her far more than she deserved, at least, that's what her mother would tell her.

"I wonder, sometimes," she said almost absently, "if my mother would have been so cruel if my father had lived."

She didn't really expect an answer, she wasn't even really aware that she'd actually said anything until Matteo spoke.

"I think, my lovely little wife, that your mother would

have been a totally different person if your father had lived. Maybe."

"I'm not so sure," she answered absently. "I think Ruby would have been cruel, no matter what. That's just who she was."

"That time of your life is over now, Marie. If you want to talk about it, I'm happy to talk about it with you. But I want you to know, it's over. You will never, ever have to live like that ever again."

She curled around him, her lips on his neck, ready to wipe her memories away with new ones. He was the perfect person for the job, she thought with a contented happy smile.

16

Matteo sat in his office, hidden away in one of the family's warehouses, and leaned his feet against the antique mahogany desk as he leaned back against the equally elderly desk chair in the office. The furniture had belonged to Nick's grandfather, the first member of the Alfonsi family to arrive in America from Italy.

The enterprising Alfonsi grandfather watched the mob back then, the Irish gangs and the Italian, that fought for supremacy in the streets of a city that continued to grow. People always wanted to escape something, back then the world wars, poverty, Prohibition, and then the Great Depression made it possible for Nick's grandfather and father to provide the citizens of New York with what they wanted most - a way to escape reality. Back then it was alcohol and cocaine that the family brought in. Then opium, hash, and even heroin, on top of bootleg gin and smuggled whiskey. The Alfonsis provided it all to those that had the money to pay for it.

The family became rich and by the time Nick came along, the desk and chair had seen thousands of days of use. Despite the wear on each one, Matteo decided to keep the desk when Celeste turned some of the reins over to him. The furniture was a testament to those men, and to the mistakes made along the way. Nick was the degenerate son that nearly lost it all, and did for himself. Celeste had saved the business, for herself and her family.

Now, the Mazzas reigned in these parts, but these days it was gambling and guns that kept the family in money.

"Boss, you in here?" A man's voice came through the door and soon a big man with black hair and light-green eyes followed.

"I'm here, Anton." Matteo sat up and pulled down the hem of his suit jacket. "Have you taken care of that little problem of ours?"

"Andy is now in Canada, shoveling pig shit at an Amish farm," Anton said, his deep voice almost loud in the empty warehouse.

"Good, and he knows that if he ever comes back, he'll find a new home at the bottom of the Hudson, right?" Matteo asked the question without inflection which made the question even deadlier.

"Yes, he knows that, Matteo." Anton came in and took a seat. His broad face, grim on most days, looked even grimmer now. If that was the look the man gave to Andy, the braggart, then Matteo knew that the point would have been made.

You don't brag about your connection to the Alfonsis, you kept it quiet, just like they did. Help these days just wasn't what it used to be.

"You going to lunch with your wife?" Anton asked and took the wooden seat in front of the desk, across from Matteo. The chair was also an antique, not meant for real comfort.

"I am. She'll be joining me here afterward." Matteo turned the laptop on his desk off and put it in his briefcase. It went wherever he did and always would.

"Very good. I'll take a ride out to one of our houses, check how things are going." Matteo knew Anton meant one of the houses "out in the country", far out of the city and generally hidden away on hills or in forests.

The family now owned, through a variety of holdings, quite a few of the old country houses that the wealthy elite used to escape the heat of the summer in the city. The houses were now places for gambling of many kinds: cards, dice, betting, even slot machines. Each house was checked regularly and staffed by trusted "managers". Anton was in charge of all of those managers and reported directly to Matteo about the goings-on in these houses.

Matteo suspected far more went on in a few of those houses, but he was about to clear all of that out, once Anton got the proof of it. One of the managers had become a bit too big for his britches, as Marie might say, and would have to go.

"You do that, and thanks, Anton. I'll see you later." Matteo left the man in his office and went out to his car, not the car Celeste had sent him to Louisiana in. He sighed as he sank into the luxurious seat and started the engine.

He drove to a place on the outskirts of the city, a quiet little French restaurant that didn't give two fucks that Yelp or Trip Adviser existed because its clientele only knew about the place through word of mouth. The word of other patrons that could afford the prices, and not just people with a few extra dollars to spend.

He pulled up to the building, a small building that looked like a log cabin made up of very dark wood. The exterior didn't matter a lot, it was the food that mattered. Dark, full of tables with white tablecloths and dark chairs, and staff that was ready and able to meet any demand waited inside, and Matteo quickly found his new wife.

He leaned down to kiss her before he took a seat across from her in the back of the restaurant lit with original gas lighting. Flames flickered along the walls and gave the interior a romantic air. She smiled happily up at him as he sat down to join her.

"Hello, darlin'," she drawled and took his hand. "How are you?"

"I'm ready to eat, Marie, and this is as close as we'll get to that lovely food I learned to love down in Louisiana. I miss the cook I had down there."

"Bring her up here then," Marie said lightly, with a soft laugh. "Or we can always go back down there."

"Soon enough, I know you must miss it. I do and I was only there a short time." He picked up the menu the waiter left when he seated Marie and looked it over. When he put the menu down the waiter came over to take his drink order.

They both ordered their food and sat with their hands entwined on the table to wait.

"How was your morning, Marie?" he asked, pleased just to be near her. He'd become used to having her in his life now, and the weeks had flown by.

They'd both calmed down after Christmas and settled into the marriage happily. It was still a surprise to him, though, how much he still longed for her company. He'd never wanted to be around anyone as much as he wanted to be with her. It was almost sappy, which he hated, but he couldn't help it. For now, he'd given in to the urge to please her, and his own need to be near her. Maybe that need would dim over time.

"I met Trina and her mother for breakfast. Audrina has calmed down a little bit." Marie sat back in her chair and tapped her manicured nails on the table. She'd chosen a dark shade of pink and black this time, and he thought it was adorable how she chose the oddest of artwork for her nails.

"You have charmed them all, Marie, I'm so proud of you." It was true, she had charmed them all. He'd seen on that first meeting, all those weeks ago at Christmas, that most of his family were prepared to absolutely hate her. They'd been polite to her, as they would be, but they didn't want to like her.

Marie, with her quiet ways and quick smile, her need to put people at ease, had charmed her way through the aunts and cousins, and now she was meeting with some of them for breakfast, on her own, without him. It was progress.

"I also looked at taking some business classes at one of the local universities. One offers a degree online, so I wouldn't even have to leave the house."

"Would you want that?" he asked as the waiter brought a bottle of red wine to the table and opened it for them. Matteo ignored the man and watched his wife.

She gave him a look that said she'd continue after the waiter left.

"Your meals will be ready in another five minutes, sir, madam." The waiter nodded politely then and left them in peace.

"It would be safer if I stayed at home, wouldn't it?" It nearly broke his heart when she asked him that.

"It, well, yes, it would be safer." He wasn't aware that she was worried about safety. He'd taken her to a shooting range to teach her how to use the gun, on more than one occasion, but he hadn't realized fear had made its way into her heart. "But, are you that afraid, Marie?"

"I'm not, not really. But it's not just, ahem, you know, *the family business*, that bothers me. The world just isn't a safe place anymore. And I'm happiest when I'm at home with you."

"I thought, after so many years of being hidden away, that you'd want to explore the world." He leaned closer across the table to her.

"I do when you're with me, or I have someone else in the family with me, but on my own? I've spent enough time alone that I long for some company more than anything.

And going to museums and shops is more fun when you have someone with you. I'm happy enough on my own, at home, but when I go out, I'd rather not be alone." She looked a little embarrassed by her admission and looked away.

"It's to be expected, I guess. Are you sure you want to join me at work, Marie?" He took a breath before he continued. "It would be alright if you didn't, you know? Aunt Celeste wants a man to take over, even though you're entitled to it, but if you want me to push I can. Or if you don't want to take part in it at all, that's fine too."

"No, I don't want to take it all from you, Matteo, and I'm not so afraid that I'd be chased away. I would like to join you though, be a part of it. Do something besides sit around all day shopping online or having lunch with the other ladies. I'm not the kind to sit around doing nothing, not for long anyway."

Their food arrived then and they both dropped the matter as they focused on the delights that earned the restaurant its reputation. Matteo watched Marie, worried about her. She seemed to be doing alright, adjusting to life in a world that was completely different from her old one, in a new place with people she didn't know. She had a slightly tired look around her eyes, a shadow beneath the lower lids that she hadn't learned to hide with makeup yet.

He decided to let her rest tonight and not keep her up until the early hours. He delighted in her, in the sounds she made as he explored her body, but she needed some sleep. He barely tasted the food, he was so caught up in watching her, but she seemed to enjoy it. She smiled happily as she put her fork down a short while later, and sighed.

"That was incredible." She wiped at her mouth with a napkin and put it down.

"It always is here." He put his own fork down, done with the meal. He'd finished it all but had no memory of eating it. All he could remember was her, the way she ate so delicately. Her mother had taught her table manners, at least. She'd even been able to pick out the correct fork at his aunt's at Christmas when the table had been decorated with an assortment of tableware. She was full of surprises like that, though.

"Do you want dessert?" he asked, his gaze on her chest. Maybe they could go back to the house for a quick… nap. He loved the way the panels of her red sweater opened when she leaned forward to reveal her enticing cleavage. His fingers itched to push those panels open and look at her beautiful body.

Then he looked up and saw her face, unguarded, and saw how truly tired she was. "Why don't I drive you home, Marie? You look exhausted."

"I'm just a little tired today, that's all. We didn't get to sleep until 3 am, you know?" A smile played around her lips, a delighted smile that held just a little hint of naughty promise.

"I do know, and you were amazing, as always." He pulled her hand to his and signaled with the other to the waiter for the bill. "You took a taxi over?"

"Yes, I'm terrified to drive in this city." She looked

down, a flush of embarrassment heating her skin. "I know you got me the new car, but, I just can't manage it."

It was a small, red sports car, and she hadn't driven it yet. He suspected she was afraid of damaging the thing, but he didn't care, so long as she could be independent and didn't hurt herself.

"We'll go out this weekend and I'll help you to get used to it. Don't worry, you'll soon be a pro at getting around traffic here." He stood up as the waiter brought their bill over in a plastic folder and then left with a wish that they come back soon. Matteo nodded at the man, paid at the cash register, and guided Marie out to his car.

Once they were in, he leaned over to kiss her. She tasted of the wine they'd shared and mint. She'd snuck one in while they were at the cash register, he guessed. "You always taste so good."

He murmured the words hotly against her lips, unwilling to pull away just yet. She pulled her face back to his and he knew it wasn't just him that didn't want the kiss to end. His hands were between her thighs, pushing up her skirt, and her breathing said she wanted him. The way she moaned when his fingers slid inside of her said the same.

There went that idea of letting her have a break, he thought, but the guilt washed away when she begged him for more. Letting her rest was going to be hard work, he thought with a chuckle as he gave her exactly what she wanted.

17

Spring was in the air and the world was coming back to life. That tended to happen in April, though. Marie looked down at the world below and saw splashes of pinks and white that weren't snow. She'd been delighted when it snowed the day after Christmas, and then again on New Year's Eve. By February, she was over her childlike excitement and saw each new flake of snow as the next drop of brownish-black sludge that it would turn to in the city.

Now, green shoots were poking up from the ground and flowers started to bloom. The world was about to bloom back into life. She sipped at her coffee and her thoughts drifted back, all the way down to the bayou, where crawfishermen would be busy trapping and families would be coming together to eat the fruits of that labor. Not that she'd ever taken part in such get-togethers, but she'd seen them from her car. Everyone smiled, laughed, and had a good time with each other.

It was a far cry from the city so far away in the north and from the family she'd found with Matteo. Matteo's family had thawed towards her, a little, well some of them had. Celeste had only made an appearance in Marie's life that one evening on Christmas Day. Trina had become a fixture in her life, though, a constant that kept Marie smiling.

Matteo and his cousin made life easier up here, where everyone sounded strange, and even the food was different. There were plenty of restaurants claiming to make Cajun or Creole food, but it wasn't the same. And she was starting to miss the quiet nights that weren't quiet at all. The road noise, the constant drone of a million machines, everything made a noise, a vibration, that came up through the floors and walls of the penthouse as a low but always present hum.

She knew it would be warmer down there, and she would be able to put away the winter clothes and break out her shorts and flip flops again. But would she? Matteo had chosen her clothes for her, basically. He'd given her a list of items to buy and had even shopped with her online to find appropriate apparel. It was only now, as she thought about her summer habit of flipflops and shorts, that she wondered if Matteo was… ashamed of her.

He was at work, at one of the warehouses possibly, and she was in the penthouse alone. She'd been happy to make sure she didn't embarrass him in front of his family, that she looked the part of a woman he could be proud of, but now, she wondered if she'd have to buy new clothes to wear in the spring and then in the summer too. Would he let her wear her shorts or flip flops?

They still hadn't said those three magic words, and she'd started to wonder if they ever would. Matteo would get this look on his face sometimes, a look that almost scared her because it looked like he was afraid. Helpless and on the verge of spilling all of his secrets. All those secrets that she could see on his face sometimes. She'd hold her breath until something in him would give, but it never did.

A wall would come down over those fascinating brown eyes, and he'd close off. The spark would fade from his face, that moment of absolute wonder would disappear, and he'd be the hard man that she'd seen him be around his aunt. The automaton that didn't feel anything.

She knew she loved him, though. She felt it keenly sometimes, so sharp it almost hurt her, how much she loved him. It was the times when he'd turn away that she loved him the most because she knew it was hurt that made him turn away. It was fear and the past that he rarely mentioned that made it so very hard for him to let himself love her.

The fact that he never saw his mother, never spoke to her, that told her what she needed to know. The hints that his mother was an alcoholic that she'd picked up from Trina, suggested something even deeper about the entire thing. Celeste took over his upbringing and from the way Trina spoke about Celeste and how she'd raised him, Marie knew that his childhood had not been a good one.

It wasn't easy to love Matteo but she'd known from the

start that it wouldn't be. Sometimes, he'd disappear for days, no explanation at all, but he'd come home eventually. All he'd want to do when he made it back was hold her. He'd come into the house, take her in his arms, and just stand there wrapped up in her. That's how she knew he loved her, every now and then he showed it, even if he didn't say it.

He made an effort to make her laugh when he knew she was down. When he could see the past was tormenting her, he'd do something for her like take her out for ice cream or to get cheesecake. He didn't see shopping as a treat, and she was glad about that, she didn't much like how much money he'd spent, even if he had bricks of it stacked in a safe at a bank. He didn't use his money to show affection, he used it to give her the things he saw as necessities. He used his humor, his kindness, and the way he always talked to her like he saw her as a person.

It was the first time in her life that Marie ever felt adored. She'd felt friendship, and even love, towards the women that came in to help her with her mother. Trina gave her friendship too, and that also made her feel like a person that mattered. But what she felt for and from Matteo was different.

She needed him, wanted to be near him, and missed him on those days when he disappeared. In the beginning, she'd been awed by everything happening, overwhelmed at his generosity, and the fact that she was not in Louisiana anymore. She was also trying to deal with far too many things at once.

Her mother's death, her whole life as her mother's

victim, a new romance, moving, being forced to marry, all of it. She sometimes wondered if she had died, not her mother, and this was heaven. She knew it wasn't, especially during those times when Matteo was gone, but still, it was the happiest she'd ever been.

She had also started some classes online, just the basics that she'd need to have under her belt to pursue a degree of some kind. She'd settled on business for the moment, but she could always change if something else caught her eye. There was time to make up her mind.

Matteo came home early that day with a gleam in his eye and a kiss for her on his lips. "Guess what?"

"What?" she asked as she settled into his arms, her body already familiar with his. She let her head sink down to his shoulder and held him close.

"We're going on a little trip. Just a getaway for the weekend, but you've been restless lately."

"That's because I have nothing to do, Matteo. Even with classes and going out with Trina, there are only so many days I can handle spas and manicures, you know? I need something to do!" She pulled away first before she turned back around. "Wait, where are we going?"

She hoped he'd tell her back to Louisiana so when he answered she was surprised.

"Miami - it's luscious in the spring. Any later than that and it will be too hot." He waited for her to show her happiness, but she disappointed him.

"Oh. That's nice." Marie turned away to hide her disappointment from him. She schooled her features into a happy smile and turned back. "When do we leave?"

She'd tried so hard to be a good Mafia wife, not to complain or make demands, as Trina had told her a good wife should be. Marie ignored the part where Trina said that's why she'd never marry a man in the Mafia and focused on what she should do. Trina let a lot slip that Marie chose to ignore, but she stored it away in the back of her mind.

Marie didn't think Matteo was a murderer, she wasn't sure she could live with a man that could kill like it was nothing. To Marie, the amount of power Matteo had was intoxicating. She'd felt powerless her entire life, and she felt like some of that power he had rubbed off on her. It made her a little independent, able to take a stand when she needed to.

"When you can get a bag packed. Just bring the necessities, we'll get what you need down there." He looked confused and stayed in the doorway. "What's up, Marie?"

"I've just got a lot on my mind, that's all." She shrugged and tried to play it off. "I have a lot of time on my hands, too much to think about, and I don't get enough time with you."

She went back to him, put her arms around his waist, and grinned up at him. "Ignore me, darlin', I'm just not myself, that's all."

"A trip will do you good then. I thought it would." He hugged her and she could sense that he wanted to question her further, but let it go. She was relieved when he nodded and rubbed his hands together with anticipation. "Let's get going, Marie. There's a place down there, fabulous food, and you'll love it."

Not as much as she'd love a bowl of seafood jambalaya from one of the family-owned restaurants back home, she thought but didn't say anything. Instead, she filled a bag with essentials, dressed in a dress that wouldn't be too hot when they got down there, and put on a jacket.

By the time they landed in Miami, she was excited to see the place. It was full of skyscrapers and the beach beckoned. "Where are we staying?"

"On a friend's yacht, right there on the water." Matteo pointed out of the window at a marina filled with yachts, unlike anything she'd ever seen.

Those weren't yachts, they were super-yachts. A car drove them down to the marina and the driver carried their bags down the dock to a boat that was more like a city on the water. Marie gaped at it as she climbed aboard and couldn't believe it.

"It's a 144-foot motor-yacht. There are ten staterooms, with separate quarters for the crew..." Matteo started but Marie interrupted.

"Crew?" She was confused. "Why does it need a crew? Is this yours, by the way?"

"No," Matteo answered with a soft laugh. "This belongs to an associate. He's loaned it to me for the weekend."

"Are we going out on it?" She sat down on one of the white leather cushions nearest to her.

"No, she'll stay docked all weekend, I just thought it would be a new experience. We can find a hotel if you prefer?" He saw a member of the crew coming up towards them and nodded.

"I can tell you, madam, that we offer some of the most

luxurious services you'll find in Miami. Anything you can find in a hotel you'll find on the *Platinum Fantasy*." The young woman with blond hair and tanned skin smiled pleasantly over at Marie.

Marie recognized the name of the boat from the script in silver on the dark blue hull of the multi-story yacht. Marie knew next to nothing about yachts but she had sense enough to know that this was a yacht that most people would never even know existed, much less ever step foot on.

"Let me show you around, then you can decide?" the young woman, with a name tag that had Tiffany written on it, added as Marie looked around.

"Oh, it's not that I don't want to stay on it, I'm just so… astonished." Marie knew it sounded unsophisticated but didn't care. It was the truth.

"Come on, let's look around."

Marie followed and saw that there were many other people onboard, quietly in the shadows working to keep everything on the yacht in order. Marie saw the stateroom they'd stay in, a large room with a double bed, television, and its own bathroom. There were quite a few decks, one with a bar and an attendant. There was a pool on another deck, along with a hot tub that caught Marie's eye. She'd never been in one and wanted to try it. They could order food from the kitchen below from anywhere on the boat and Marie realized they didn't have to leave it for anything. It really was a city on the water.

"We could just live on this boat forever, Matteo," she said once they were alone in their room. She sighed happily and looked over at him. "I need a bathing suit, maybe even a bikini."

She grinned at him happily with a naughty tilt to her lips.

"That we can arrange, just find one online and I'll have someone go and get it for you." He sprawled out on the bed and gave his own sigh of happiness. "I'll need a few things too, and later we'll go out for dinner."

"Oh, but we could just stay here…" Marie sighed out as she came to lie beside him. "It's so fascinating."

"The food will be worth taking a step away from the yacht for a while."

"It better be." She took his hand in hers and looked over at him. "Thank you. I was going stir crazy back home. You really have to find something for me to do."

"But I don't want you to work, you don't have to."

"Oh," Marie responded softly. "But I'm used to staying busy, Matteo. This is really hard for me you know? Not doing anything all day."

"Do you want to be a Mafia Queen or something?" He looked over at her with a grin. "What could you do? What skills do you have?"

She was a little miffed at him for dismissing her, but she forgot about it as she turned over towards him. "I have one skill that you can't live without."

Her hand slid down between his pants and his skin. His eyes went wide and a smile stretched over his face.

"Oh yes, you do have some very good skills that I very much adore." He pushed his zipper down and opened his belt to give her easier access to the parts of him that she was most focused on.

With a whisper of a groan Matteo lifted his lips to hers as she began to stir them both into a passion that was never far away. She wanted to tell him about how much she loved him but kept it to herself. That was for another time, someday in the future.

A wave of dizziness made her skin go cold and she gripped at him. She felt as if she might fall out of the bed, but when she held onto him, she steadied again. Maybe it was just seasickness, she thought and took a deep breath. His lips brushed against hers and Marie forgot about the moment, too caught up in her husband to let the moment be ruined.

18

A few weeks later Marie put her laptop down and leaned back in her chair. She was at the kitchen table where she was studying, the sun going down. The sky hadn't gone completely dark yet, though, and Matteo would be home soon. They were going out for dinner, so the oven and stove weren't on.

She'd taken her laptop to the kitchen, where she usually studied, and had been sitting in the hard chair for hours now. In between studying for school and writing papers, she was catching up on what it meant to actually be a mob wife. Yeah, she'd had talks with Trina, but she wanted to go deeper.

Some might say that she was seeking out the truth about her father, and in a way, maybe she was, she decided. She only knew her mother's side about what kind of man her father was. She didn't know about his life from those spiteful venomous words, just that her mother hated him. Marie wanted to know about him but the one woman that could tell her the most about him hated her. Marie had only met her the one time, but she knew when she was hated.

She'd felt that same cold hate from Celeste that she'd felt from her mother. It left her unsettled even now when she thought about it. Celeste was not an avenue for information then. The only way she could get to know him, and by extension, Matteo, was to study other Mafia families.

The truth was obvious about the reality shows she found online to watch; these were people being paid to make drama. She moved on to documentaries and then began to read about the subject. She saw things that horrified her, that took some of the glamorousness out of her fantasies about what this life was about. The truth splashed her with cold water, and Marie sat in the kitchen of the penthouse apartment as the minutes passed in a stunned state.

Matteo could be a very dangerous man and if she wasn't careful, life could be very short. Not from him, she doubted he would ever truly physically hurt her. He could destroy her emotionally, that was definite, but not physically. Frustrated now, she got out of the chair and picked up her phone.

The only people she had to call were Trina and Matteo. She needed other friends. Or a group of some kind to join. She'd seen a lot of groups at the school's online website, maybe she should find a group that actually met and got together.

Then she thought about something that had been niggling at her. Matteo never went out without a gun on him lately. He seemed stressed too, distracted when he was at home. Something was bothering him, but she wasn't sure what it was, because he didn't talk to her about those things.

He talked to her, that wasn't the problem. It was just that he didn't talk about his day, his feelings, what was bothering him. She wanted to change that but had no idea how. And now, after the research she'd done, she doubted she'd ever get her future Mafia king to ever talk to her about the business.

Despite the warnings she'd read that afternoon, she wanted in the family business. She brought the subject up an hour later as they sat at dinner in a very expensive Mexican restaurant. Matteo had just revealed the family owned the place and that beneath their feet a casino was ramping up for a night of gambling.

"Look, I know that me becoming involved in the business is something that takes trust. Nobody knows me, nobody trusts me, except you maybe, but can't I do something down there?"

"I don't know." Matteo blinked at her, unsure of what to tell her.

"I'm not well educated, I know that, but I'm a good observer. I'm a problem-solver and I'm eager to learn. Surely there is something I can do?"

"I'll find something, Marie, I promise. I'm not sure what we can have you do, but if you really want it this much, then, I'll find something." He shifted in his chair and pushed away from the plate that had been filled with steak fajitas not long ago but was now empty. The motion revealed the gun snug up against his left side with a holster, and Marie's eyes shot up to his.

"And maybe take me for more shooting lessons?" she said the last part quietly, afraid to say it too loudly in the restaurant that was only now starting to fill up. They'd got there at the right time then.

"Yeah, I'll take you out in the morning, alright?" He tipped his finger at the waiter who quickly rushed over and asked what he could do for Matteo.

"Another glass of white wine for my wife please, Andy, and a small port for me please." Matteo was always kind to the staff, wherever they were, which was another reason Marie loved him.

People that were rude to the people that served them at stores or other places of business irritated Marie. They were snobby and that was more than Marie could tolerate. In her younger days, when she could still get around, Marie's mother would go out into town and would talk condescendingly to everyone she came into contact with. She would be rude on purpose, just to get a rise out of them, because she knew if they reacted, they'd get fired. Even if it was Ruby Hebert they were rude to.

"Do you want to go downstairs?" he asked after they finished their drinks. His eyes were bright with delight. "I'd love to show you off."

"I've seen how you growl at any man that comes near me with the least hint of interest," Marie quickly retorted, amused.

"Showing you off is one thing, having men make an

attempt to hit on you is something totally different," he said with a dry smirk and a raised eyebrow.

"Ah, so you want them jealous, that's it?" She got up from her chair, her bag in hand, and waited for him to escort her to wherever the door was for the place.

"Always." It was an admission that shocked her. Not because he wanted men to be jealous of him, but that he'd actually admitted it.

A smile tilted the corners of her mouth as he led her back to the kitchen, and then to a room where wine was stored. His fingers traced along the wall until he found a button and pressed it. A thick steel door slid to the left side slowly and she saw a set of dark stairs.

"Wow." She breathed as they descended the stairs, and she saw a large number of people gathered around tables and machines. Alcohol flowed from a bar off to the left while the gambling stations were to the right and towards the stairs.

"This place was built during the 1920s, during Prohibition. A speakeasy. I bought the restaurant above so that I could have this below. We keep it quiet, for obvious reasons, and anyone that comes in has to become a member. That keeps them quiet because they know we keep a member list. There's no advertising and people can't talk about the club. It's private and members only."

"What about those women?" Marie pointed to a group of women around a table full of men playing cards.

"They can bring their women in, but there's no prostitution here, and we don't provide that kind of entertainment." He patted her hand and looked down at her as they paused at the bottom of the steps. "I'd never do that to a woman or allow it. I've fired a couple of managers at some of my houses lately, for that very reason."

"I'm glad." She tried to think quickly, to come up with something to keep him talking but her brain went blank. "I'm not sure they are those men's wives."

"I doubt it, but I can't ask them, either."

"Doesn't that break the privacy rules?" she asked as the thought occurred to her.

"It does, in a way, but each guest has to sign a privacy form. Besides, these people know that they are exposing others to gossip, so they don't bring in anyone that would break our policy. It keeps them happy too."

"And those women?" Marie asked as she spotted a table full of women playing cards at another table.

"They're some of the biggest names in the business, but you won't ever hear about them. They don't play the regular circuits, only the underground places." Matteo led her to the bar and ordered two coffees for them after she told him what she wanted.

Marie watched the women at the table, fascinated by the fact that women were playing. She knew women could, but she'd considered this to be a man's world and had thought women wouldn't be involved. It was nice to see the group over there. One was a tall woman who looked to be about 45, with short blond hair and bright blue eyes; another had black hair and brown eyes; while the last one had long gray hair, wearing sunglasses, and sweats. The other two women were dressed all in black, clothes that looked expensive, but weren't meant to.

Marie looked down at the spring-inspired dress she had on. It was light pink with a wide white belt across the middle. The short cap sleeves were enough to keep her shoulders covered. It was a modest dress but... girlish. Those women looked like they meant business. She pulled her lip between her teeth and watched them. Even the woman in the gray sweats looked tough, capable. Not like a mousey housewife that would be more at home at a church luncheon than down here in an illegal casino.

"What do you think?" he asked and took a seat at a table they'd walked to.

"I think it's fascinating." She wanted to go to another store, right now, and buy more new clothes. Clothes that said she meant business, like those women over there. Maybe then Matteo would take her seriously.

"I'm glad you like it. It's my own pet project, not one of the family's businesses." She looked around with a new understanding. He'd built this up himself, with his own money and efforts. He wanted to show it off to her.

That made sense now.

"You want to have a play at the machines?" he asked and took out a bundle of cash from his pocket. "Try some of the machines, if you want. You can learn some of the table games from those."

"Oh, okay." She hadn't expected to play any of the games, but she soon discovered she liked them. It was all chance, and she was sure the machines were rigged in the house's favor, but it was fun. When you had money, she reminded herself.

"Having fun?" he asked a little while later. She'd won

$200 by then and didn't want to stop.

"Yeah, but it's addictive, isn't it?" She picked up her winnings, put it in her bag, and put her hand in his.

"It can be, yes." He didn't look at her and she knew that was the thing about this business. It was meant to be addictive, otherwise, nobody would play. It was all about luck and how much the odds were in your favor.

It probably wasn't a good idea to think about that too much, she decided as they drove away a little while later. Then you'd feel guilty and she didn't want to feel that. She had enough to feel guilty over.

When they got home, Matteo took her to bed, undressed her slowly, and touched her so softly it was nearly heartbreaking. He spent hours worshipping her, or so it felt like. When they finally rolled together to go to sleep she was exhausted, in love, and content.

"You gave me the world. You make me feel like I'm important, and you want to make me happy. I never expected all of this you know? My biggest plan was to buy a camper van and travel around the country until I found a new place to call home."

"You weren't going to stay in Louisiana?" he asked and she could tell he was confused.

"Why would I? You saw the funeral, there wasn't anyone there. It was going to be like that for the rest of my life. People would ignore my existence unless they were forced to speak to me for some reason. They hated my mother, she was damaged goods which meant I was damaged goods, too. I didn't want to stay somewhere I wasn't wanted. I was hoping to find a place where I could make friends, have a nice quiet life, and live the rest of my days without all the judgment."

"So, a small town somewhere, huh?"

"Yeah. I mean, I miss it. I miss the nature there, the bayou and the wildlife. I miss home sometimes, the familiarity of it all, but I'm building a life here." She sat up against her pillows and looked over at him. "I'd like to go back one day, but I'm not in much of a rush. For a while, I missed it dearly, but I'm getting used to living up here."

"Do you want to move to a place somewhere out of the city?" he asked and looked like he was open to the idea.

"No, not right now. I like it here. I feel like I'm safe on top of the world." She slid down a little and leaned over to kiss him. "I'm safe anywhere you are, and that's the most important thing. I don't care where I am now, as long as you're there. There's no need for that camper van anymore. I have a home now, you gave me that."

"It's not a perfect home, though. Are you sure you're happy here?" He stroked a lock of hair out of her face and kissed her softly.

"I am, Matteo. It's wonderful."

"Not quite, but I think you'll make more friends as time goes by. It'll turn into a small town before you know it, believe me." He kissed her again and rolled to his back. "Now, let's sleep. I'm going to get you up early to have that lesson."

She grinned and turned her bedside lamp off. This really was perfect she decided. What she'd said was true, she had a home and it lived in Matteo. Wherever he was, was good enough for her.

19

Darkness crept along the street as Matteo drove up to his aunt's house. His fists clenched on the steering wheel as he stopped the car. She'd called him, summoned him really, that morning and he'd been able to defer the meeting until the end of the day. Now, he had to go in there and pretend he didn't care about anything she said.

He took a deep breath, got out of the car, and strolled up to the door. His jaw clenched as he opened the door and waltzed in. He didn't bother to knock this time or wait for the doorman, he just went in, because this time he was alone. She'd dress him down, brow-beat him, he'd nod his head and go home.

He'd wondered when this summons would come and now that it had, he felt relief mixed with anger. Celeste spent a lot of time in Italy now, she was confident in Matteo enough that she left matters in his hands more and more. But she would question him over his decision to marry Marie and he knew it.

That relief didn't stop the way his eyes narrowed, or how his nostrils flared as he thought about Celeste and how she ignored Marie. There were no more dinner invitations, no attempts to reach out to her, and that was a snub in Matteo's mind. He stalked through the house, up the stairs, and flung open the door to the office Celeste preferred.

"I'm here," he announced as he went to the drinks cabinet and poured out a measure of whiskey.

"I'm glad to hear it." Celeste's voice came from the darkness around the desk to the left of him in the large room.

She must have a migraine, he thought, something that happened often. That or she wanted to hide her features from him.

He sipped at the whiskey while he settled himself on the couch and watched the haze that came from that darkness. The acrid scent tickled his nose and he turned his head to inhale fresh air. She was smoking again, something she did when she wanted to appear confident, in control. She used the cigarette, the way she held it, the way she'd jab at the air with it, and the way her eyes would narrow as she inhaled, to underline points she wanted to make.

He hated the affectation, but it was effective. Or it had been before he met Marie. Now, he felt more in control of himself, more capable of dealing with Celeste. There was someone in his corner, at last. His own mother hadn't protected him from Celeste, or the life she set up for him, but Marie would. Not that he needed protection now, but he'd needed someone to be on his side, he just hadn't realized it until Marie came along.

"You know, Matteo, that I'm not happy with you right now, right?" Celeste's raspy voice came out of the darkness, and an image flashed in Matteo's mind.

Some fictional movie character with all the power, wheezing out of the darkness about how much control they had, even as they lost it. It made Matteo snort and he heard her heels hit the floor as she sat up.

"I raised you up out of nothingness, Matteo, a life of mediocrity, and you snort at me?" Her voice shook as she tried to control her outrage. He didn't care.

"Look, Aunt Celeste, I did what I thought was best for all of us. You sent me down there to take care of an old debt and to get the heat off of me up here. Heat I did not bring down on myself I'd like to note." He paused and took a deep breath to calm the racing of his heart. He'd never defied her, or spoke over her, like this.

"I sent you down there to humiliate Ruby Hebert, to break her!" A crack filled the air as Celeste slapped at the top of her desk. Her face came into the dim light cast by a floor lamp behind Matteo.

He grinned as he saw the way her left eye twitched and her mouth pursed into a tight line. It was a very dirty grin, one of complete triumph. He'd made her angry, good.

"You dare, Matteo? You dare to smirk at me? You were sent to Louisiana to deal with Ruby Hebert. Instead, you marry her waif of a daughter and humiliate your family!" She pounded on the desk with her fist again, a move that upended several items on her desk, including a vase full of roses. The vase crashed to the floor and shattered into sparkling shards of broken glass. Water flooded onto the hardwood as the roses fell to the floor, discarded.

A bit like their relationship, that shattered vase, Matteo decided. It had once been a relationship of beauty, a beauty that hid thorns encased in a delicate container that could break quite easily with a little pressure. He inhaled slowly and looked up at her with narrowed eyes.

"Aunt Celeste, I will do my duties to this family. I will ensure every member of our family is taken care of, and I will continue my duties to you. I would remind you that you raised me, you, not my mother. You taught me to think, to look ahead, to do what is best for this family, and when I made a judgment that could be of benefit to this family, you question me? I'm surprised you'd question yourself like that." He leaned back against the sofa that was too small to contain his height, at ease now, as he relaxed into the cushions.

"You dare…," her voice choked off and she looked away, pulling back into the darkness with a soft hiss that was the only sound she could get out at that moment.

He waited, no longer afraid of the woman. He hated to admit it, but he'd lived his life in fear of her. Until Marie came along and showed him that he was worth something, that he was capable, and that being under Celeste's thumb had turned him into her whipping boy his entire life.

"I'll continue to be your lackey, Aunt, don't get all riled up and have a stroke." He sighed as he stretched his legs out, totally comfortable now. "I'll be whatever you want me to be, but I also want a little bit of respect. You want me to take over this organization and be the boss when you retire, but you don't want me to act like it? I made a decision about my future, the family's future, based on what *you* have taught me. Think about that before you ask me how I dare."

Silence was all he heard. Then the sound of acrylic tapping against the desktop, slowly at first, then faster as her agitation grew. Matteo could only continue to smirk and wait. She'd either have someone come in and shoot him, or she'd get over it. He wasn't afraid she'd shoot him because he knew she'd never shot anyone. She always had someone else come along to do the dirty work for her. Someone like him. Not anymore.

"Fine, Matteo. Fine. But know this, I will not treat that young woman as a member of our family. I will not accept her as anything but what she is - my dead husband's bastard child." She remained in the darkness, but he could almost feel the waves of defeated anger coming off of her, even from his place on the couch.

Matteo nodded, gently, but his hair still fell over his forehead. He flicked it away and stood up. "Is that all?"

"No. Trina tells me she's formed a friendship with the young woman. That she's... *nice.* I hope that won't weaken you in any way?" Celeste leaned forward and her eyes narrowed avidly as she examined his features.

His shoulders blocked the light behind him now, but he could still see her face, the way her lips twisted, and her chin jutted forward in distaste. She wasn't just angry, she was furious, but also bested. He'd beaten her at her own game for once.

"I'll be fine, Aunt." He spoke calmly, his deep voice a vibration that buzzed in the air.

"See that you are." She leaned forward and he saw a flash of sparks as she stubbed out her cigarette. "I won't tell you what I truly think, but I will say I don't see this marriage ending well, for any of us. You chose wrong. I'll leave it at that. You may go."

Just like that, she dismissed him - done with him, for now. He turned and left the room, quietly closing the door as he made his exit.

That went better than he'd hoped. Dread had turned his stomach into knots for months now as he waited for the summons that he knew was coming, but now that it was over, he felt… better.

A lot had changed since that first moment when he laid eyes on Marie. He didn't like the way she made him feel, not at first, because he took it for weakness. Any sign of caring for another human being was something your enemies could use against you and should be avoided at all costs, that's what Celeste had taught him. Now? Now, he liked the way she made him feel.

He was her protector and that gave him power and a purpose, unlike anything he'd had before. He would do whatever it took to keep her safe, to give her happiness, and to make sure the light stayed gleaming and bright in her eyes, even if that meant defying his aunt. He'd defy the world for Marie.

Matteo glanced down as he got into the car to drive

home. His hands shook as his heart raced and the blood surged through his veins as he thought about her. He might just love that woman, he realized. He wasn't sure he was actually capable of something such as love and happiness, or maybe even… having a family of his own.

No, he wasn't ready for that, not babies and diapers, and doctor appointments. No puppies or kittens, or even turtles and hamsters. Not yet. He was only now getting used to the idea of having a wife.

She was sitting up in the bed when he got home, ready with a hug and a kiss as he sprawled out beside her. "How did it go?"

"Well, she may have a contract out on me now, if that tells you anything." He tucked the tips of his toe into the back of the shoe on his other foot to kick it off before he did the other one. She'd kill him if he got dirt on the bed, which was something else that was new to him.

He was a clean person and wouldn't be happy if he got dirt on the bed either, but she fussed at him. Actually *fussed* when he did something without thinking that would make a mess. It was adorable to him that she did it. He knew a lot of men complained about their wives nagging at them about their shoes, or making messes, but he loved it. She cared about their house, their home, not just him, and that meant she was happy with him.

"I'll scratch her eyes out if she does." She rolled to him, her leg over his as she looked into his eyes. The way her eyes narrowed and her jaw went tight told him she was serious, but then she grinned to wipe the thought away. "But I doubt she'd do that. She needs you, Matteo. Otherwise, she'd have thrown her fit long before now. She's been plotting I'd guess, trying to figure out how to get rid of me and has decided she can't."

"I think Trina might have had something to do with that. She said Trina told her you were nice. So, she probably also told her you're stuck with me because I'd walk through fire for you and even my cousin can see it." He pulled her close to lightly press his lips to her as he wrapped his arms around her waist. "Anyone could see it if they just looked at me when I look at you. I'm sure it's written all over my face."

"Maybe." She tucked her face into his neck, something that always made him shudder with pleasure before she finished. "I just know that I'd do the same, so I think we'll manage to deal with your aunt, somehow, won't we?"

"I think so, baby. Now," he paused to slap her bottom gently before he pushed her away, "do we have brownies and ice cream? I'm starving but I don't want dinner."

"I had dinner earlier. I'll see if we have some brownies, I think we have cake… Woah!" Marie fell back into the bed, her hand against her head as she gave a faint cry of distress.

"What's wrong? Marie?" Matteo rushed to sit up and take her in his arms as she rolled to her side. Frantic, he pushed her hand away from her face, his eyes wide and his mouth open to ask more questions.

"Sorry, damn, I'm sorry, Matteo. I'm fine. I just stood up too quick, that's all. A little dizziness, it'll pass." Her voice shook, but when she opened her eyes they were clear and focused directly on him. "I'm just tired, baby, don't panic."

"It's my job to panic." He ran his hands down her arms

as he leaned over her and made sure she was still all in one piece. "What was that about?"

"I'm just tired, really, that's all. I didn't sleep well last night and I was busy today. I had a paper to research and write, and then I was out with Trina for dinner. Which doesn't sound like a lot, but going anywhere here is an adventure, isn't it?" She sat up slowly and put her palm against his cheek. "See, I'm fine?"

She didn't fall back again or wobble so he let her up. "Fine, but I'm coming into the kitchen with you."

"Good, you can tell me about the rest of your meeting."

He watched her as they walked into the kitchen and saw her gait was fine and she didn't stumble at all. Maybe it was as she said, and she was just tired. It unnerved him though, the thought that she might be ill. The power of that worry unnerved him too. Maybe he really was in love, in real love. That shook him even harder, but he hid it behind a can of whipped cream he took out of the fridge and sprayed directly into his mouth. That made her laugh and that was the best medicine in the world, for anything, he decided. The sound of her laughter made everything better.

20

*M*atteo's finger hovered over the mousepad, what used to be his stomach now a hard lump that ached in his abdomen. Celeste had emailed him and he didn't want to open it. He reminded himself he wasn't a coward and clicked the button to open the message.

"You can have your little mouse, Matteo. I've thought about it and maybe marriage is a good idea. The woman is beautiful, after all, just like her mother used to be. Marriage gives you an image of wholesome respectability, a family man. It also seems to have given you the backbone to stand up to me, at last. I take that as a sign that you are ready. I'm going to Italy for 6 months. During that time, you will rarely hear from me. The family business is yours to run as you see fit. But, remember, this is only a trial. If there are problems I will come back and take control. I wish you the best of luck. Until next time... Celeste."

He stared at the email, speechless, really speechless, for the first time in his life. She was leaving him in charge?

Two days had passed since he'd gone to see his aunt. Now, here she was, with her subtle dig that Marie's mother had ruined her marriage and a little hint that she thought Marie would age as badly as her mother had. Matteo knew her mother had lived a hard life, though, and that she'd had a disease that ravaged her body and her mind. Besides, Marie's looks weren't the only thing that attracted him to her.

He closed the email, poured himself a glass of whiskey, and left it on a side table by the couch. It was time to be a king. And the first thing this king needed was his wife.

One final swallow and the glass was empty. He left it on his desk as he walked out of the room, his arms swinging to take off the blue suit jacket he still wore. He threw it on a chair as he walked by. He removed his cufflinks and pulled the white shirt away as he walked in bare feet to the bedroom. She was in bed reading one of her textbooks. The moment she looked up and saw his bare chest in the doorway she let the book fall to the floor and slid down into the covers over her legs, a broad smile on her face.

"Hello darling, ready for bed, are you?" she asked him and stretched out in a way that subtly pushed her breasts up high in the air. He couldn't wait to get those in his hands or to run his palms down the long length of her torso.

"Hmm, yes. But tonight, I think we should do things a little different…" He drawled the words as he went to his dresser. He put the cufflinks down before his hand moved down to a drawer to pull out several long silk scarves. Each one was black and long enough to be used for several purposes. From the look of delighted curiosity on her face, he knew she knew what he had in mind.

"Oh? And will I get a say in this?" She answered her own question by staying right where she was, stretched out, with her wrists over her head.

"You always have a say, baby. But if you want to play, then I suggest you take off that nightgown and roll over." He noted it was one of the nightgowns he'd specifically bought for her - a thin, white cotton gown that bared her shoulders and only came down to her knees. It was meant to look virginal, but on her, it became a mixture of virginal and sultry.

Even now, her eyes glowed with a heat that told him she was more than ready to play his games. Those eyes took on an air of defiance as she pulled the gown over her head, threw it away, and then rolled over onto her stomach, the covers pushed to the other side of the bed. She turned her face to watch him as he walked over to her.

His vision narrowed down until all he saw was the long length of her body stretched out on the bed. He gazed at her long, slim legs that filled out to form her hips, then up to the lush mounds of her ass that narrowed to form her waist, then, the length of her back, her spine a path that led him up to her face. A step forward and the focus became her face. His heart rate picked up, but he controlled his breathing, determined to make this last.

Her dark eyes were shuttered as he tied her hands together then looped the silk around one of the posts on the bed. Not so much that her arms would be up in an awkward position, but enough that she wouldn't be able to move too far away. When he moved back he saw the shutters had gone and now there was a burning need in their place.

He leaned over, close enough to kiss her full hot lips, but he spoke instead. "Ready for this, baby?"

"I'm always ready for you, Matteo." The words came out as a sigh of bliss.

"Good." He climbed onto the bed, over her hips, and settled down to massage her neck. His fingers pushed deep into her muscles to help her relax. She gave a moan of pain that calmed into a groan as he worked at the knot he'd found. His fingers moved slowly down her back, exploring her one inch at a time. He was hard, the zipper of his trousers caused him a tremendous amount of discomfort, but he ignored the pain. For now.

His fingers began to stroke lower, along her sides, where they brushed against the firm outline of her breasts. She sighed then and that nearly undid him. The feel of her silky skin against his fingertips was distracting, but he stayed on course. He moved down her body, working out a dozen knots of tense muscles before he reached her ass. There, his fingers delved down, to find her already wet and ready for him.

All he'd done was massage her, but she responded as she always did to him. He didn't even have to touch her sometimes, just being near him made her wet and that was more intoxicating than any drug he might have experimented with back in his younger days. The fact that Marie wanted him that much made his head spin because it matched his need for her.

His right hand traveled up her spine and slid into her hair, while his left stayed in her cleft, exploring the slick heat there. With his left hand, he slid two fingers into her sultry depths while his right gripped at her hair to pull her head back.

"Tell me what you want, Marie." It was a demand, not a question.

"I want you to get me off, Matteo." She knew better than to deflect now, she knew to state what she wanted clearly.

His fingers moved inside of her, into her, deeper, before he pulled out. He pulled at her hair just a little tighter, just enough to make her his with excitement. She knew all she had to do was tell him to stop and he would, but she didn't.

"And how do you want me to do that, Marie? Do you want me to finger you until you break? Is that what you want? Or do you want me to fuck you, baby? Tell me how you want me to get you off."

"I want it all, Matteo. I want everything you can give me." Her eyes were open as she spoke, but he didn't think they saw anything. She was too attuned to the sound of his breathing, to what she could hear behind her.

He fucked her with his fingers until those eyes closed and a shudder ran down her back. She was close.

He let her hair go and moved down to sit between her thighs. He pulled at her hips to snug her up against his hard cock. It was a torment for them both, but he could handle it. Marie, on the other hand, couldn't, and he chuckled when he saw her fingers clench on the silk that bound her hands together.

His fingers moved faster as he bent over her, his breath a feather whisper across her ass when he spoke. "Tell me you need me, Marie."

"I do." She was too caught up in her own pleasure to pay attention, to say anything that long. He paused the movements of his hand, even though she was on the edge, even though she groaned in protest. He denied her what she'd denied him, satisfaction.

He needed to know she wanted him, liked him, maybe even loved him, but neither of them was ready to say words like love. He'd settle for her need. To know that she needed him made something inside of him unfurl from its prison, something that he wanted to release but had never been able to.

"That's not what I fucking asked you, Marie. I asked you to tell me you need me." His lips kissed the place where her ass met her thigh before he pushed her legs wider and leaned into the secret scented garden that was only his. He knew he owned her, body and soul, she'd shown him that more than once, but he wanted to know she wanted that ownership, that she needed it to be him and only him.

He needed something of his own and that something was her.

"I fucking need you, Matteo," she answered with a sigh of pleasure when his lips found her folds. "I need you to take me to heaven. I need you to make the world disappear, darlin'. I need you, all of you."

"Do you need all of me inside of you?" His tongue came out to split her open, to slide down to the button that would set her off. He pulled her up on her knees to get better access. "Or do you need my tongue on you, Marie? Is that what you need? My tongue beating at your clit until you fly into a million pieces?"

"Yes," was all she could answer when his tongue found that button again. Her sweet sounds of delight made his skin hot, the essence of her on his tongue made him sweat while at the same time his cock pulsed.

He twisted a fist in the sheet on the bed as he worked to make her make those sounds that unleashed that something inside of him, that something that only she could bring out.

"Matteo," she moaned his name, her hips twisting in time with her rapid breaths. He could feel how hot her skin was as he moved his hands to grasp at her thighs, to spread her even wider. "Matteo, I'm so close…"

He pulled away then, completely, and moved off the bed. His pants disappeared and he climbed back up onto the bed.

"You know, Marie," he paused to run a finger up from her feet to the back of her knees. He heard her moan, watched as her toes curled back towards her feet, and smiled with a smug delight that he'd tickled her. His fingers stroked at the delicate skin at the back of her knees before they moved up to her thighs. He moved up behind her and began to stroke at his cock as he looked at her.

Moisture glistened on her thighs and he wanted to taste it, to lick it away.

He'd become distracted. He stopped the movement of his hand on himself and he focused on her again.

"Sex isn't always about the rush to the end. Sometimes,

it's about…" he paused to move his hand to her pussy, to the spot they both were focused on. His thumb slid in her wet juices until he plunged it into her. When her hips jerked and she moaned, he spoke again. "Sometimes, it's about the fun of getting there."

He pulled the thumb out of her, edged it around her skin, over her clit, before he moved it back down to her entrance. She moaned, she made sounds of protest, but she didn't tell him to stop. Instead, she twisted her hips to encourage him to go further, to let her have that escape she needed. But she was his, he'd tell her when she could get off.

"What do you think, Marie, want to ride my hand and tongue until you get off, or should I fuck you into the next world?" He purred the words against her clit and he thought for sure she'd pop off, but her back arched, her ass clenched, and her voice drifted to him, harsh and thick with her desire.

"I don't know, Matteo. You're the one in control here, aren't you?"

The little fucking tease. That nearly ruined him, and he had to breathe through his nose for quite a long moment to regain control, to not break. She'd nearly taken control with that statement, nearly pushed him into giving her exactly what she wanted, but he just smiled grimly and ran his hand down her leg, to curl along the arch of her foot.

"I am, indeed, Marie. Now, tell me, how do you want it? Or do you want it all?"

"I want everything, Matteo. All of it. But only with you." She looked back at him, her neck craned in a way that must be painful, but in the dim light cast by her bedside lamp, he saw her eyes. Her cheeks were flushed a bright red and her hairline was damp with sweat. She was beautiful, gorgeous, and then she broke him.

All she did was run her tongue over her dry lips, but he got an image of her tongue on his cock, and that snapped the very thin cord that held him to his control.

With a groan of surrender, Matteo pulled her hips up to the right angle and slammed into her. This is what she wanted, the brutal fucking beast that made her his, that made her forget the world, but what she didn't understand was that when she pulled that beast out of him, he became hers.

He was totally, completely hers and the world didn't exist anymore. Just them. The past didn't exist anymore. All that there was was this moment, her, and him. Nothing more.

"Nothing," he whispered raggedly as a pulse of pleasure ripped from him and that ragged whisper set her off with him.

Together they flew apart. They rose into the universe as nothing more than the essence of themselves, and when they came back to Earth, they reassembled as one. Nothing could tear that apart.

21

Marie waltzed out of the lobby of the building and out to the street to slide into her cab. It wasn't something she'd have ever contemplated doing a year ago, but there she was, sliding in and greeting the cabby with the address she wanted to go to.

The driver gave a thumbs up and pulled out into traffic with practiced ease. She could have driven, but her nerves were shot and she couldn't handle NYC traffic today. Not today.

Her fingers tapped at her phone in her lap, the cover closed. She wasn't sending a message, she was just... nervous. She took a deep breath and stared out at nothing as the car sped away to the address she'd given.

She was worried about a few things. Things that plagued her. Lethargy kept her home and she'd missed a nail appointment already because she couldn't get up the energy to go to the appointment. Her normal appetite had all but disappeared and her frame had become slimmer. Then there was the dizziness that wouldn't leave her be.

She hadn't told Matteo about any of it and when he came home she pretended she was fine. More than once she'd forced herself to get up off the couch and go out with him, to dinner, or a function that he needed to attend. It was torture, though, and left her even more exhausted than she already was.

Her visit to the doctor was to confirm what the pregnancy test had revealed - she wasn't pregnant. That had been her first thought, that she was pregnant. It would explain everything, but the pregnancy test she'd bought on a trip to the store alone had put a big ole nope on that idea.

Marie wasn't sure she could trust the test though, they weren't always right. Worry nagged at her, and there was one thought she pushed away over and over. Her mother had been tired, very tired a long time ago. The woman that normally went out dancing, drinking, and whatever else it was she did. The woman that could get up the next day and do it all over again with exuberance had one day stayed on the couch. That had been the beginning.

That wasn't what was wrong with her, she reassured herself as the cab pulled up to the building she'd directed him to. Her mother's disease wasn't genetic, not necessarily. She was just tired, stressed from the events of the last eight months or so of her life. Life had thrown a lot at her at once and she was having trouble coping. If she wasn't pregnant, then that was all that was wrong with her. She knew it.

A few moments later the cab drove away and Marie

walked into the lobby of the doctor's office. She spoke with the receptionist and took the clipboard filled with page after page of forms for her to fill out. Marie's hand ached by the time she finished and returned the paper.

By the time her name was called Marie's brain had slipped into pause mode, that place where we all seem to go to when we have to wait and we're bored. She jerked up out of her seat with a stiff smile on her face and walked up to the shorter woman that looked at her expectantly.

"I'm Marie Mazza," she told the woman whose nametag had "Anne" written on it.

"Hi there, I'm Anne. Can you step up on the scale for me, please?" the younger woman, probably five years younger than Marie with light brown hair and pretty blue eyes, asked.

Marie went through the ritual of health checks and was taken to a room. The nurse left shortly after and a doctor came in.

"Hi, Marie, I'm Doctor Murphy. How can I help you today?" He was an older man, somewhere around sixty, with calm brown eyes and a gentle smile. His eyes searched her over, hidden behind a pair of black bifocals before they came back up to her eyes.

"I'm a little worried about a few symptoms I've had lately." Her voice cut off and she looked down at her hands. Her thumbnail tapped out a beat on the other one as she tried to pull her thoughts together. "I thought I was pregnant, but I took a home test and it was negative, so I thought I'd best see a doctor."

"Tell me what your symptoms are," he asked, his brows

knitted together as he sat down in a chair across from the examination table she occupied. He crossed his legs and put his clipboard on the raised knee as he waited.

"I'm tired, mostly. Very tired. I don't want to eat, I'm either nauseous or not hungry. Sleeping has become a battle over the last few weeks." Ever since the night Matteo's aunt sent him that email and left for Italy.

She had another symptom, but she thought it was better to show him so she held out her hands. "And there's this…"

Her nails were polished now and her long, slim fingers were held straight out. A moment after she put her hands out it happened. A slight tremor that made her pinky twitch, and then her entire hand trembled. Her right hand and then her left.

"I see. Do you have any neurological problems? Any damage to your spine or neck?" He wrote down a note and stood up again. He asked for permission to touch her and she agreed.

His hand worked along her neck and down her spine before he moved away. "I don't see anything there. But there may be something else there. Can you tell me when this started?"

"A few months ago. It was just this silly twitch at first." She pointed up her pinky finger on her right hand. "Have you looked at my family history?"

Her head was down once again, afraid to see anything in the doctor's eyes.

He cleared his throat before he answered. "I have, and I have to say, I think you have valid concerns, Marie. I'll order a pregnancy test and a few others. Don't worry," he paused to reassure her with a calm smile, "we'll get to the bottom of this."

"Thank you, doctor." The smile she sent back to him was wobbly, and her eyes were damp. "I'm just worried, you know?"

"I understand, Marie, I do. Just let me reassure you, stress can cause all of these problems, and I don't think there's a soul alive that isn't stressed these days. Can you tell me how things have been going at home lately? I saw in your file that you used to live in Louisiana. A beautiful place, what brought you up to this jungle?"

"I got married," she said simply. She began to elaborate, told him about her childhood, about her mother, her mother's death, the marriage, and by the time she'd finished he nodded sagely.

"I think you've just told us the main reasons for your current problems, Marie. You've had a lot of trauma. A lot." He frowned as he wrote another note on his clipboard. "I want you to think about getting some counseling, alright? While we wait for these test results."

"Oh," she said simply, her eyebrows raised. That wasn't something she'd considered at all.

Her relationship with her mother had been chaotic, and the rest of it. Well, maybe the doctor was right. He had a calm manner that made him seem competent and able to make decisions like this. The advice was sound, it just wasn't something she'd ever considered. Counseling? That was for crazy people, wasn't it? Basket cases that couldn't help themselves.

That's what her mother had told her. She'd come home from one doctor's appointment and complained about the doctor that had told her that her symptoms were all in her head and she just needed to see a shrink. Marie had sensed it was the doctor's dismissiveness that bothered her mother, but she'd also understood the words. Psychiatrists were for nutcases, and Marie wasn't nuts. But, maybe she did need some help coming to terms with everything that had happened.

"I'm not dismissing you, I hope you understand that Marie?" He waited for her to nod yes before he continued. "Good, because that's not it at all. Whether you were having these symptoms or not, after what you've just told me, I think it's best for you. And like I said, I still want to run some tests, just to be sure about your physical health, alright?"

"Yes, Doctor Murphy, thank you." She looked up with a pleased smile. He'd listened to her, heard her, and that was important. Now, she had to find a way to tell all of this to Matteo. She'd hidden it all, worried that she would end up like her mother, that he'd divorce her. Or that he'd wrap her in cotton and never let her out on her own again.

He was so protective of her, she knew that if she'd told him about her problems, he'd go overboard. For now, she wanted to be calm, wanted to not be wrapped away from her own problems. She wanted to face this now that she'd turned her face towards her fears.

"I'll wait for the pregnancy test results, and if that's negative, I'll write you some prescriptions. A sleeping tablet that you can take when you can't get to sleep, and another to help you relax. Only take them when you need to, alright? They are habit-forming."

"Of course, doctor. Thank you."

The doctor left her in the exam room as he went out to check on another patient. The nurse came in to take blood and urine from her, and 30 minutes later Marie left with the prescriptions the doctor mentioned along with a referral to a counselor. She took a deep breath, certain now that she wasn't pregnant.

Now, she just had to wait to find out what the other tests revealed. For now, she was glad she wasn't pregnant. She wanted a child with Matteo, she'd decided, but in the future. Not right now, not when she was just getting to know herself and him.

Over the last few months, she'd found out a lot about herself. Without her mother there to henpeck her, she'd found she loved looking pretty for her husband. She found she was brilliant at school and her grades showed that. She'd found confidence and independence that she hadn't realized she lacked.

Her mother was dead, and yes, she was conflicted about that; sometimes she felt heartless because she was glad to be free of her. At other times, she felt... free. Like a bird that had been let out of a cage that flew away, free to sing and explore the world it had been denied.

The cage she'd lived in had been invisible; her mother's hatred of her a cage she couldn't escape. She'd tried but she'd failed. She'd been too weak back then, too afraid, to leave her mother to her own life. Someone could have come in to care for her mother, more PCAs perhaps, or she could have been put into a nursing home. But Marie had been afraid, afraid and hopeful. A small, childish part of her had hoped that her mother would come to love her. That her illness would soften her and make her see how devoted Marie was to her. But that hadn't happened, and Marie had continued to live in that prison of hope and fear.

Now, though, she thought with a shake of her dark brown hair, she could do almost anything. She had a husband she loved and desired, she had a home, a life, a future. Even if she was on the path that had taken her mother's life, she decided, she would live the time she had with happiness.

There was a smile on her face as she held up her hand to hail a cab. The green and black maxi dress she had on billowed around her legs as she waited, a triumphant figure that probably appeared to be nothing more than a woman hailing a cab to anyone else. But to her, she knew she was the perfect image of a woman that had truly become free at last.

Sure, she had some trauma to deal with, but there was help out there. And she had Matteo. He would be a rock for her, no matter what. She knew that as well as she knew that once he got over his need to wrap her away from the world, he'd see the logic and be the companion she needed.

She gave another address to the new cabbie and when she stepped out into the late spring sunshine, sunlight glinted off of her dark hair to create a red halo around her face. A woman standing at the curb gasped as she saw the effect.

"Marie, you really are beautiful, do you know that?" Trina came up to hug Marie and lead her to a café they'd agreed to meet at. "I can't believe it sometimes, and then there you are in all your loveliness. How are you?"

"I'm good, a little tired, but it's been a long day already. How are you?" Marie took a seat at one of the empty tables and picked up the menu. She looked over at Trina, though, to wait for her answer.

"I'm fine, as always, Marie. What are you having?" Sunlight gleamed from Trina's dark gray eyes, made them lighter and glint with the shine of silver.

Marie's smile stretched a little further. Trina was lovely, too, even if she didn't think anything of it.

"I'm going to go for something healthy, maybe a salad." She glanced down at the menu to study it.

"Why, you're not pregnant are you?" Trina's eyebrows were raised in a hopeful way, her face wreathed in a smile.

"No, but I'm a little… I don't know how to say it. A lot has happened, and I've just been told I need to take some time to heal from it all. And I think that's good advice. Step one is healthy, eating, right?"

"Right." Trina nodded and looked at the menu. "I'm here for you, you know? I know I'm part of the family, but I'm not like them, okay? I think you're great, and a good friend. I'm here if you need anything."

"I know you are and thank you. The same goes for you." Marie smiled, even if Trina couldn't see it as they both stared at the menus they held.

Trina had never been pushy about information, she'd always listened, and though she didn't know about Marie's childhood, it was like she could sense there was a pain in Marie's heart, and treated her with respect. That was all she'd ever asked for, to be treated with respect, so Marie gave the same to Trina.

The future was uncertain, but Marie knew one thing, she wasn't alone anymore.

22

Marie washed her hands once she got home and started to make dinner. Cooking was therapeutic to her and always had been. She had her favorite music on and hummed along to it as she prepared the food. She had decided it was time for something familiar and cooked the onions and bell pepper for a jambalaya that would start the dish.

A bell at the door told her she had a visitor. They rarely had visitors, so she wondered who it was. She looked out of the security hole in the door and had to take a deep breath to calm her suddenly racing pulse. With her hand on the knob, she exhaled and tried to tell herself to stay calm.

The very last thing Marie needed was to open the door and see Celeste with a sneer on her face, but there she was, sneering away. Marie schooled her features into a look of calm and tilted her head up slightly to look at the other woman.

"Hello, Marie, is Matteo home?" She waved her be-ringed hand at the doorway as if to tell Marie to move aside, but Marie stood her ground.

"No, he's not, Celeste. Can I help you?" Marie leaned into the doorjamb, just to make sure the other woman was positively certain Marie wasn't going to invite her in. Marie didn't trust her any further than she could throw her.

She looked Celeste over, dressed in some kind of black 1920s suit, right down to the wide-brimmed black hat tilted to the left. Like some kind of gangster's moll from back in the day, Marie thought. It was attractive, but the pencil skirt that flared out at the knees wasn't for her.

Celeste took a deep breath, tilted her head to the right, which made the hat move in a way that amused Marie so much her lips twitched. "Look, I don't like you. I don't like the fact that my nephew married you. But you are his wife, so I have to tolerate you. Can we call some kind of truce?"

"I suppose we must." Marie moved out of the doorway and stood to the side. "Please, come in."

"Thank you." Celeste waltzed in on black heels no woman in the 1920s would have been able to afford. Marie couldn't tell which designer they were but knew they were if they were on those feet.

"Can I get you a drink?" Marie walked back to the kitchen and tightened the belt of the light-green full-length silk robe she wore. Beneath it, she wore a matching night-gown with thin straps and a short hem.

"Scotch if he has it." Celeste followed her to the kitchen and sat at a stool at the island.

Marie moved to one side, poured a small glass of scotch, and a small one of gin with tonic for herself. She turned to the island and stood in front of it as if the barrier would protect her from Matteo's aunt.

"Did you even go to a university, Marie? Do you have any kind of education?" Celeste looked her up and down and continued. "I can see why he's taken with you, you are beautiful in that dark, gypsy kind of way I suppose."

Celeste sniffed as if the air was bad and her upper lip curled with distaste. "You must be fun in bed, otherwise he wouldn't be so in love with you. But your mother was, so I suppose you will have inherited her talents. Or your father's, he was a good lover too."

Marie stared at the woman, her eyes wide with shock. Who was this bitch to insult her like this in her own house? "Excuse me?"

"What else would explain Matteo's adoration of you? Your intelligence? Your sweet nature? No, men fall in love with one thing and once it ages a little, well, you're a prime example of what happens when you get older."

Marie could have sworn the world blacked out for a minute as her blood pressure pounded in her ears. She gripped at the island, her knuckles white as she tried to contain herself.

"From what I understand, your mother said much the same thing to anyone that would listen, though, didn't she? That men only wanted one thing and when they were done with you, they'd just throw you away? Yes, the report I got before I sent Matteo down told me quite a lot about you both. It just didn't explain how well you'd seduce my nephew into your bed."

"I think you'll find it was the other way around." Marie sipped at her drink as cold rage washed over her, calmed her nerves, and left her with the ability to think clearly once again. "With your husband and Matteo."

"My husband was a cretin that let his dick lead him around. I raised Matteo to think with his brain, not his dick. It seems one whiff of you changed that." Celeste raised her glass and sipped at it, her eyes still narrowed with distaste.

Marie scoffed, amused at the woman's gall. Marie might not be a Mafia queen, but she was a grown woman, and she saw this display for what it was - an attempt to dominate her and make her afraid. To show any kind of fear would be a mistake with this woman, though. Her head rose a little higher still and she was all but looking down her nose at Celeste now. "Jealous?"

"What?" Celeste looked at Marie with eyebrows raised in astonishment. "I beg your pardon?"

"The way you're carrying on, Celeste, one would wonder, you know? Why is she concerned with who her nephew sleeps with? What's driving that?" Marie leaned over the island as she spoke, her cold anger apparent in the tight smile on her face. "Wouldn't you think so, Celeste?"

"I'm not, that's ludicrous!" Celeste exclaimed and pulled away from Marie. "I've never heard such drivel."

"Then I suggest you stop worrying about who Matteo sleeps with. He sleeps with me, and I'm his wife, that should be all you need to know." Marie took another drink of her gin and tonic and then looked at Celeste again. "You aren't going to play nice at all, are you?"

"No, I don't think I will, Marie. I don't want you to be his wife. You aren't quite what I had in mind for him. I'll get rid of you, or he will when he gets tired of you. He thinks he loves you right now, but that will fade with time. Thank you for the drink." She set her empty glass down and looked directly into Marie's eyes. "Tell my nephew I'm leaving tonight. He has six months to prove himself. Then I'm done."

Marie watched her with cautious eyes, waiting for a glass of acid or a gun to be pulled on her. Neither happened and she relaxed as the woman walked out of the kitchen. "Have a nice trip, Auntie."

She said it to be a bitch and when Celeste's foot faltered, she knew she'd hit her mark. Celeste was not as impervious as she made out then. Good.

"Goodbye, Marie. I hope we don't meet again." Celeste turned back with a cheerful grin on her face, her hands on the door as she walked out of the penthouse, but Marie knew it was a lie. It hid the scowl that hid behind the façade Celeste now tried to keep a hold on.

"I hope for the same, safe travels, Auntie." Marie's smile was more pointed than Celeste's.

Inside, Marie was a roiling wreck of "holy fucks" and "don't say that", but she didn't back down and gave as good as she got.

"Tata." The older woman gave a weak wave of her fingers as she walked out of the door and closed it.

Marie sank back against the door, her fingers fumbled

to lock it before she slid down to the floor, totally spent, shocked, and… happy.

There were other emotions in the jumbled up mixture that went through her mind. Fear, anger, desperation, but there was also happiness. Celeste believed Matteo was in love with Marie. That was a good thing, even if Celeste didn't like it.

There was also the idea that she'd just bested Celeste at her own game. So, there was pride in that mixed bag of emotions, too.

"Fuck," Marie breathed the word out and pushed herself up from the floor. She had dinner to make, a husband to welcome home. She blinked a few times as she stood up, her heart still pounding, but it all started to calm down she finally felt after a few moments.

Her own mother hadn't wanted her, she thought as she walked into the kitchen and downed the rest of her drink. That she was aware of, perfectly aware of. Celeste had wanted Matteo, but she did not, she most certainly did not, want Marie in his life. Would she ever be good enough for anyone from that generation?

She put the glasses in the sink to wash and got back to her jambalaya. Celeste's little visit brought up memories from the past, the way her mother would sneer at her, the way she'd scream at her, that she was unwanted. It made her shoulders droop, and her head just didn't want to come up.

She'd scored a few direct hits with Celeste today, but it was a quiet wife that greeted Matteo when he got home. It was a woman that couldn't escape the past, not right now.

"Hi, darlin'," she said with a kiss as he walked into the kitchen a few hours later. "Dinner's almost done. I'm just taking the bread out of the oven."

"It smells like Louisiana in here." His broad smile was pleased and he nodded his head. "Good. I'll change and meet you at the table, okay?"

"That's fine." She wasn't sure whether to tell him Celeste came by or not. How would he react? He didn't like the woman any more than she did, she'd sensed that from the first mention of his aunt. Would he want to know she'd been here?

She put the jambalaya into bowls, some warm bread in a basket, then carried it all to the dining table. She knew it would taste fine, she'd made it a million times before, but she also knew she wouldn't taste a bite of it.

She poured gin and cold tonic water into a tall glass and took it to the table. Her focus was on that glass throughout dinner, and she re-filled it once. Fucking bitch and her mind games, she thought as she started on the second glass. Well, fourth, but she'd started the count over once she sat down for dinner.

Marie wasn't much of a drinker, but the entire day had left her rattled. She thought about the pills she'd hidden away in her nightstand. Should she tell him about those? She didn't realize he'd noticed, not until he spoke.

"What's wrong, Marie?" He sat back in his chair, his eyebrows pulled down with worry.

"What? What do you mean?" She looked over at him, her fingers on the glass, her eyes on the bowl of food in front of her. She couldn't stomach the thought of it right now. Maybe she did need one of those pills after all.

Not with the alcohol, that's what the bottles had said anyway, it would intensify the effects. Her thoughts had already drifted away, to a time when her mother had her down on the floor, scrubbing it with a toothbrush and gritty Ajax. The fact that her mother's fingers were gripped in her hair and her voice screamed at Marie wouldn't stop replaying in her mind. It mingled with that sneer of Celeste and she just wanted to curl up in a ball and cry. But she was a wife now.

"That. That right there." He pointed at her. "You keep spacing out. You're drinking gin, which I didn't even know you liked, and you're… not right. What's wrong, baby?"

He reached across the table for the hand she held the glass with and she let the glass go reluctantly. She didn't want to tell him anything right now, she felt too fragile, like she was in too many poorly held together pieces and the slightest pressure would shatter her completely.

But why, she tried to figure out. Why did she feel like that? Shouldn't she be proud of herself, shouldn't she feel like she'd won a battle?

"I'm just not feeling well, Matteo, that's all." She smiled at him, but they both knew it was fake. She stood up, gathered up their dishes, and took them into the kitchen to clean. She washed everything up while he stood behind her and told her about his day.

Well, the parts he could tell her, she thought, because even Matteo kept secrets from her. That was alright, though, she decided later when she was curled up against his sleeping form. A mafia queen she was not and today had proven that.

She thought about that referral to a counselor and decided she'd give them a call. She needed to. She needed help or this would only grow worse. She knew enough about trauma now, she knew about depression and PTSD, all those things that the internet now made a thing that was out in the open, that you could read about freely. She'd done some reading about it when she first got home that afternoon, and as she rolled over to stare at the drawer that held those pills, she reached out her hand.

She didn't open the drawer, not yet, she'd had a drink and worried she'd make a mistake. No, for now, it was enough to know they were there, just in case. She brought her hand back and tucked it under her cheek, but her eyes wouldn't close. In her mind, moments replayed, words suddenly decided to repeat, and she felt the torment all over again. Tears slid down her cheeks as she sobbed quietly into her pillow.

Fuck Celeste. Fuck her mother. Fuck them both.

She swiped at her eyes, got up out of bed, and went into the living room. She found a movie on Netflix, muted the volume, and read the subtitles until she finally fell asleep. Reading the subtitles distracted her enough to let her go to sleep, at last. Alone on the couch.

23

"Good afternoon, Senator Carmichael," Matteo said the next day, his hands on his desk. "Good to see you."

"You too, Matteo, you too." The senator put out his hand for Matteo to shake so he took it from the rather large man with dark circles under his eyes. The puffy skin beneath those cold green eyes reminded Matteo of dough that had been left to rise too long.

He hated the senator. He'd got Matteo into trouble in the past, and was one of the reasons Matteo had to go to Louisiana to get the heat off of him. It was his nephew that had done all the bragging about being a gangster. That wasn't why Matteo hated him, though, that was the man's own lack of morals that bothered Matteo.

Matteo had had to bribe a few law enforcement officers to get the rest of that heat off of himself, and his family, but he'd done it gladly. Now this bastard was here to fuck it all up, he just knew it.

"What can I do for you, Senator?" Matteo leaned back in his chair at another office, this one an office for the construction company they used to launder money. This office had a newer desk and a much newer chair, far more ergonomic than the antique one at the warehouse office.

"I need a favor, Matteo. My other sister's kid is trying to get up in the scene you know? He wants into the game, and he has a plan. A plan that involves you." The senator's eyes stared at Matteo avidly, and Matteo could see the greedy way the man licked his lips and breathed, which was very hard for a man of the senator's size. Matteo could hear the way the man's pulmonary system strained to work under all of that weight and it made his eyes narrow.

The senator was not a healthy man, and he could hear it. That wasn't good, not when the man was here to ask for a favor.

"He's got some product coming in from Columbia, good stuff, I promise. More like the old kind we used to get you know?" The man looked at Matteo and seemed to realize his mistake. "Well, you may not remember it."

The man gave a short laugh before he looked down at his nails, polished perfectly to a healthy shine.

Matteo sat passively in his chair, waiting for the man to get to his point.

"I've heard you don't have any, ahem, product, in your casino at the Mexican place."

"And I intend to keep it that way," Matteo said and sat forward, his eyes narrowed with suspicion now. He knew exactly what the senator wanted now. "Forget it, it's not going to happen."

"Hear me out, Matteo. We're talking about five million dollars worth of the stuff." The senator sat forward, his chubby hands now on Matteo's desk. Matteo didn't like that and glared at the man's hands until he pulled back.

"Listen, I don't care if it's worth 20 million, Senator. Your last nephew nearly finished me, is this one going to complete the job?"

"Strange that, isn't it, Matteo? How he disappeared like that." The senator's voice was quiet now, threatening. Like he had secret knowledge that should make Matteo afraid.

"Not really," Matteo answered with a nonchalant shrug. "The boy left our organization and ran away to newer pastures. Maybe he went down to Mexico to get away for a while?"

Matteo's raised eyebrow of warning didn't deter the senator. "Well, you see, Matteo, his mother doesn't think so. And neither do I. Now, I can push for an investigation, maybe try to find her son for her, but there's my other nephew, you see? He needs a little helping hand. Maybe think about it for a while, before you turn it down out of hand?"

The senator sat back as if he'd just won a rather challenging game of chess, his smile one of self-assured pride. Matteo wanted to punch it off his face. He had enough on his plate, right now, there was something wrong with his wife. He didn't need this prick in here with his weak attempts at blackmail.

"Try it, Senator, and your wife, along with the media, get those pictures you seem to have forgotten about. The ones that were taken with that male prostitute with the many lines of coke he was snorting off your ass? Remember those?" Matteo leaned forward, a dangerous glint in his eye.

The Senator swallowed and gibbered for a moment before he could form words. "I thought you'd burned those."

"Some of them, Senator. Some of them. I'm not a stupid man, you understand?" Matteo's left eyebrow rose over his eye, a threat to the senator that he needed to shut the fuck up and listen.

"Ah, yes. I see. Well, have a nice day, Matteo." The man scuttled away as fast as his heavy frame would let him and Matteo leaned back into his chair again. That was easy enough, he thought. Now, if only he could crack what was wrong with Marie so easily.

A knock came at the door and the green eyes of his main man in New York appeared in the doorway. "Boss, we got a problem at the Green Valley house. One of the men brought in a hooker and the two of them are causing a problem."

"Great. Just what I needed. Let's go, Anton." Matteo pulled his suit jacket off the back of his chair as he stood and followed Anton out of the door.

"What's the problem?" Matteo asked as Anton drove his Audi out of the city and onto a highway.

"She's screeching about wanting coke, it's not even 10 am yet. But anyway, she wants it, he hasn't got any, and we don't provide it. So, she'd wandered around until she's found some paint in one of the outbuildings. Splashed it all over the entranceway, and then hid in their bedroom. She won't come out now."

Just what he needed, a cokehead without a fix. He really needed to get home to his wife, but business came first, right now. He'd found Marie asleep on the couch this morning, tear tracks streaked down her tanned cheeks. She caught the sun, even when she wore a hat, poor thing.

What bothered him wasn't the tan though, it was the tear tracks and the fact that she was on the couch. Was she unhappy with him? Surely, she'd say something? He worried over the matter the whole way up to Green Valley, a place a couple hours outside of the city.

He hadn't come up with a solution by the time they sorted the matter and got the woman to come out of the room. Anton tipped a tiny bottle of coke under the door to lure her out. Not their usual policy, but at least the man had the sense to know it would be the only thing to get her out without breaking the door down.

Matteo wanted out of the drug trade completely. He never wanted to see any of it again, but he knew he couldn't escape it. Not with his life choices. The woman left with the man finally, and Matteo waved them away. He had a maintenance guy come in to clean up the smeared paint and paint over what he could and checked the rest of the staff at the place. He reminded them all that it might be a gambling joint, but it wasn't a drug den. He didn't want any of his staff carrying at any time. If they were, it was grounds for dismissal.

"I don't care how much money you can make off the clients that come in here. You bring one speck of coke, or anything else, into this place, and you're finished. Understand me?"

They'd all nodded before he sent them all back to work.

On the way back, Matteo finally realized they'd listened to Johnny Cash the entire way up to the house. He couldn't do two more hours of it, though. "Man, I like Johnny, but can we have something else?"

"Sure, boss. What you want? I have it all." He tapped the expensive player in the dash of the car and Matteo tapped at buttons until he found some Beatles. He let *The Long and Winding Road* fill the confines of the car and finally began to relax. He loved the song, but not many people knew he was a Beatles fan.

The song played out as they merged onto the highway and Matteo began to relax. He was tired, he'd spent a lot of time at work lately, in the car, traveling between all these damned houses, and it was wearing him down. He just wanted to go home and relax with his wife. She needed him, he could see it, but he'd been so busy lately.

Tonight, he'd make an effort to get her to talk. She'd become accustomed to bottling things up, to packing them away, with her mother, but he knew some of those closets were packed full, they had to be. She needed to talk to someone and he wanted that person to be him.

He bought a new bottle of gin and a couple of limes before he drove home. He'd get her drunk and let her slur it all out. It worked for men, right? It might not be the best idea he'd ever had, but it might let her blow off some steam, at least.

"Baby, I'm home." He smelled her version of fajitas

drifting in from the kitchen. Tequila might have been a better choice, but she seemed to have developed a taste for gin that he'd appease.

"I'm in here, Matteo." She wore a bright smile when he came in and he could see she was a little better today. She didn't look as haunted as she had the night before.

He leaned down to kiss her hello and lingered for a moment. "I have a plan for tonight, my luscious little honey. We're going to listen to music and get completely smashed together. I've never seen you drunk, and for some reason, I'd really like to see that."

"Think I'll be amusing, do you?" She grinned and twisted like a happy puppy in his arms before she pulled away. "Okay, but let's eat first."

He didn't want to mention anything that might put her off the idea, so he didn't tell her she might not want to barf up fajitas later. He wouldn't let her get that far, he decided. Just enough to get her talking, and maybe giggle.

They washed up the dinner dishes together after they ate, then he made them both a drink. "Let's go into the living room. Let me take you on a journey."

They both laughed at that as she did as he instructed. She settled down on the couch and grinned when he handed her a drink with a green umbrella in it. "Oh, now that's professional."

"I give only the best to my woman." He raised a finger and pointed in the air before he moved to the sound system. "Now, let's see."

"What are you going to play for me, dear husband of

mine?" She grinned and he could see it was genuine when he glanced back at her.

"Something you may not have heard. Come here, dance with me. I'll teach you if you don't know how, don't worry. Come here." He beckoned to her as the song began to fill the air.

"It's *Stand By Me*. But I don't know who's singing it. Is that John Lennon?" She swayed with him and moved her body to the short but lovely song. "That was beautiful, play it again."

He obliged and hit the back button on the remote control. He began to sing along as the song played and Marie stood away from him. He could see she was stunned and gave a rueful smile. "What?"

"Replay. Now. And sing that for me all over again." She sat down on the couch, her drink now in her hands.

He didn't want to, but she insisted. He did it, and though he felt self-conscious at first, he got into the song as it carried on.

"Matteo, your voice is beautiful! Why don't you sing?" Her eyes were wide and her smile showed just how impressed she was. The raspy sound of her voice told him how amazed she was. He felt his cheeks go warm, and he looked down at his feet.

"I used to, back when I was in school. My aunt had other plans for me, though. I don't do much of it anymore." He thought about the guitar hidden away in the closet and had an idea. "Just a minute."

He retrieved the guitar and brought it out into the living room. "Fill our glasses back up and sit down."

He arranged a chair in front of her, played a few chords to remind his fingers how to move on the frets, and then he began to sing to her. No singing over another voice this time, it was just him and the guitar. He sang a few songs he'd written himself and when she clapped her hands, her eyes wide with glee, he felt a new pride start to warm its way through his chest.

He refilled their glasses while she gushed over his performance.

"I hate it that I'll be the only person to ever hear those songs, Matteo. You have to record those somewhere. You really do."

"Nah, I don't have time for all that." He waved her praise away and came back to sit down with her. He hit play on the sound system and let a new song play. "I have you, work, and you. That's all I need."

"Then do it for me. I'd love to be able to play that when I need to smile." She leaned into him and he put his hand down on her thigh, just as a way to touch, not as a prelude to something else. Sometimes it was nice to just sit and talk to her.

"Would it make you smile when you're sad, Marie? Really?" He looked over at her, serious for a moment.

"It would. That song was beautiful, Matteo. Lonely, but full of hope." She turned her face away. "I think we both know about being lonely, don't we?"

"I think so. You haven't told me a lot about your life, but I can guess." Matteo sipped carefully at his own drink. He wanted her to be the one that was smashed, he wanted to be there for her while she was.

"No, you can't." Her head rolled away as if her neck bones were made of liquid. She was getting there, then. She was on her fourth glass, though.

She began to talk then, to spill so many secrets that she'd never told him before. By the time she was done, he wanted to go back to Louisiana, resurrect her mother, and throttle her. Marie had fallen asleep on his lap, tears staining her cheeks, but at last, she'd got it out. He picked her up, carried her in his arms, and took her to bed. She'd mentioned a counselor at some point there, said something about a doctor appointment yesterday. Maybe it would be a good idea. From what she'd just told him, she needed to talk to someone with professional skills he didn't have. He'd be right there for her, though, every step of the way.

24

$\mathcal{M}$atteo kissed Marie goodbye and she went into the bathroom to get ready for her appointment. She'd set up a spa day with Trina, an attempt to relax, as suggested by the psychiatrist she'd seen a week after her doctor appointment.

The woman was nice, had listened to what Marie had to say on their first appointment, and had suggested they start slow. She wanted Marie to practice some relaxation techniques and do everything she could to relax. Matteo had agreed, which surprised her.

She'd woken up this morning, after he'd decided to get her drunk, with a slight hangover and the distinct memory of spending hours telling him about her childhood. He was supportive and stayed home the next day to make sure she was alright. They'd spent some time talking about it all throughout the day and had come to the decision, together, that counseling would be good for her.

After a shower and drying her hair, she got dressed in

casual clothes: a light-blue skirt that billowed softly around her knees and a white silk camisole. The clothes wouldn't be on her for long so she went for something she could slip off and on easily. A pair of flat sandals replaced the flip flops she was used to wearing.

For a moment she stared down at her feet. The sandals were a camel-brown leather with gold and turquoise beads along the panel that stretched across her feet and around the strap that ran around her ankle to close on the outside with a gold clasp. When it was warm in Louisiana, she'd pull out her old flip flops and carry on. Sometimes, she'd splurge a little and buy a new pair at the closest discount store.

Now, she could afford fancy sandals and that fact took her breath away. She didn't have to wear flip flops, even though she was used to wearing them, but she could if she wanted to. That was the difference in her life, she could choose what she wore now. With a hint of a smile on her face, she left the penthouse and went down to the car she'd decided to drive.

The sunlight glinted off the windshield of the white Fiat Matteo ordered for her when she pulled out of the parking garage. It was a small, compact car, and though it was rather boxy, she loved it. She just had to get used to driving in New York traffic. That part wasn't so easy, but she was getting the hang of it.

She turned right as she pulled out of the garage and came to a yellow traffic light. She braked just as the light turned red and waited for the green signal. The car was quiet, so she turned her gaze to the radio and had just started to flick through the buttons when a pinging sound made her look up.

There were men in black standing 200 feet in front of the car, they'd surrounded it, and every single one of them wore black ski-masks. Marie froze, her mouth as wide open as her eyes were as she took in the fact that each man held a handgun in his hand, all pointed at her.

Stupidly, she glanced up at the light and wanted to cry when she saw it was still red. She looked down and saw that one was drawing closer. Her brain went into automatic then and said fuck the traffic light, she had to move. She stomped her foot down on the gas just as the gunman started to fire, and his companions joined him.

Bullets sprayed into the car, the windshield starred so badly she could barely see, and each second felt like an eternity as the car began to move forward. The men moved as she drove by, but the shots being fired did not stop. Something stung her side as she drove by a group to her left but she ignored the burning pain as she tried to get away.

What the fuck was happening? She couldn't figure it out, and at the moment all she could really focus on was her escape. The side mirror to her left was gone, the windshield was cracked and in fragments but still holding steady in its frame. She tried to see through a small section about two inches wide as the car sped forward, but the pain in her side started to sting even more and she felt her panic turn into a rope around her neck that grew tighter with each moment that passed.

Her thoughts turned to Matteo when she saw that the

men were far behind her. She needed to call him, but she couldn't take her eyes off that two-inch section of the windshield for long and she was afraid to take her hands off the steering wheel. She wasn't sure what the shots might have damaged in the car and she was worried it would stall before she could get to… where? The spa? No, not there. She needed to go somewhere safe. She saw a white sign with a blue H on it and finally glanced down at her side.

A startled cry of fear and surprise tore from her throat when she saw the entire left side of her camisole was covered in red. Blood. That was blood. Holy fuck, that was blood. Another sound of distress broke the silence in the car and her foot came off the gas pedal. She realized she'd slowed down when a car behind her blew its horn and she glanced up startled. She'd taken her eyes off that two-inch section for too long and she was about to run into a light pole.

She put her foot on the brake, but she didn't do it fast enough. With the sound of screaming metal in her ears and fear crushing her heart, Marie braced for the impact. She hit the pole at 45 miles per hour. An airbag exploded from the steering wheel and threw her awkwardly back against her door just as the back end of the car swung around and tilted over. Marie's head slammed against the window as the car crashed down on its side. Blood continued to pour out of the wound in her side, a warm trickle of her life slipping away, she thought just as the world went dark around her.

* * *

"MARIE? MARIE, CAN YOU HEAR ME?" A stranger's voice called to her from somewhere outside of the darkness and she tried to open her eyes.

It felt like her eyelids weighed a ton as she tried to open them, and she whimpered in distress. Why couldn't she open her eyes? She whimpered again as she tried as hard as she could to force her eyelids to open until finally, they opened up just enough for her to see the face of a man dressed in a fireman's uniform, right down to the yellow helmet he wore. "Ma'am, can you hear me?"

"I… I can." She tried to lift her hand but she was too tired. The struggle to open her eyelids had sapped her strength. What was wrong, what had happened? Why was she on the street with a fireman kneeling over her. "What's happened?"

"Ma'am, it looks like you've been shot and then hit a pole. We're taking you to the hospital, you're safe."

Marie tried to nod but her head was so heavy all she could do was let it fall to the side. That showed her the car, peppered with gunshots, and she wondered how she'd survived. Pain lanced through her head as a wave of nausea covered her skin with gooseflesh. The wrenching burn of pain was all she knew as the agony in her side suddenly became too strong to ignore, too much to bear, and the world went dark again.

* * *

"She's coming around," she heard Matteo whisper near to her and she reached out for him, fear stealing her voice away. All she could do was make an odd sound as she reached out to him, for him, and she opened her eyes to look around. Where were they? Where were those men with the guns?

"It's alright, baby, I'm here. Don't worry, you're safe and I'm here. Those men are gone." He slid into the hospital bed beside her and took her gently in his arms. "Don't move, alright, Marie? You've had to have one very epic surgery and you're going to be here in the hospital for a while. Which is probably the safest place you can be right now."

"What surgery?" she whispered, not sure why anyone would do surgery on her.

"You were hit on the left side. The bullet severed a section of your intestines and the surgeon had to put it back together and clean up the area around it. It's been dealt with but you're not out of the woods yet. They want to keep you in to watch for infection and to make sure you won't need another surgery." He took a deep breath and ran his hand down her right arm. "Baby, I'm sorry. You were apparently targeted for an assassination attempt. I don't know why yet, but that's what it looks like. The police are investigating, and you'll have to speak to them in a few minutes, but for now, I want you to know, I'm handling this. They will be taken care of. Keep that in mind when you talk to the police, alright?"

"I will," she said carefully. His voice had been gentle when he spoke, but there was a deadly undertone to it that she couldn't ignore. "I'm not scared, anyway, Matteo. You're here with me."

She squeezed his hand gently and then put her head back on the pillow. "I'm so tired. I want to go back to sleep."

"You can after you talk to the police, honey. Come on now, have a sip of water, and let the nurses look you over first." A pair of nurses dressed in rose-colored scrubs came into the room.

"How is your pain, Mrs. Mazza?" the nurse with rich, dark skin asked as she leaned over the left side of the rail of Marie's bed.

"It's not bad. I don't feel much, to be honest." She gave the gentle-looking woman with a cut chin-length bob a tentative smile.

"Good, your medicine is working then. May I check your wound?" She waited for Marie's answer patiently, and when Marie nodded in response she pushed the covers down and pulled up Marie's hospital gown to check the bandages that now covered her stomach. Her hands were covered in purple gloves and it made the touch less personal and invasive, at least to Marie.

She turned her head away from the nurse to look at Matteo. She didn't want to see the wound right now, not until she'd absorbed all of this. She'd been ambushed and shot at, the same way her parents had been all those years ago. For the second time in her life, once before she was born but alive in her mother's body, and now outside of the cradling protection of her mother's body, she was part of an assassination attempt.

This only occurred to her at that moment. She'd lived her entire life without that realization, but it came home to her now while she allowed a nurse to check her gunshot wound.

"The wound was made bigger when the surgeon opened you up, Marie." The nurse spoke softly, in a way that reassured her patient. The other nurse took notes and wrote down Marie's vital signs. "The doctor will come down soon and explain things to you better, but for now, you're safe and we have you in our hands. We won't let anything else hurt you, okay?"

Marie turned back to look into the woman's dark-brown eyes and felt an urge to cry as tears welled up in her eyes. "Thank you."

"You're welcome, honey." The nurse patted her arm, removed her gloves, and sprayed a shot of alcohol foam on her hands. "Your wound looks good and there's no redness. "Your temperature is good too, no fever. You're doing really well, considering."

"I'm glad. Thank you. You've really made me feel so much better." Marie wasn't sure why, maybe it was the motherly attitude the woman treated her with, but something about the woman calmed her and really had made her feel better.

"I'll be back later, but there's a button if you need us," the other nurse said with a smile that reached her light-gray eyes.

"Thanks," Marie answered and then settled back into the bed.

A few minutes later a knock came at the door.

"Mrs. Mazza, I'm Detective Boyd. I'll be investigating your case. How are you feeling?" The 40-something man in a cheap black suit with thin black hair came into the room. He had hazel eyes that looked directly at Marie as if she was a bug he wanted to examine.

That made her bristle a little, but then he smiled. "Sorry, I can be intimidating to people sometimes. I was just trying to get a handle on you. Do you feel like answering a few questions?"

"I guess I have to, don't I?" She gave him a defeated smile that soon turned to a straight look of strength. She could do this.

"Can you tell me anything about what happened?"

"Where do you want me to start?" Marie asked as she tried to think. She could remember everything up until the car hit that light pole. After that, she couldn't remember anything.

"Well, can you tell me how many gunmen there were?" The man took out a phone and started to tap into it. The modern-day replacement of the notepad she guessed.

"I was at the stoplight, about to turn the radio on, when I heard a pinging sound. I looked up, saw the men, and I hate to say it, but I panicked. I think I ran the red light." She looked down at her cracked manicure, one nail was jagged and needed to be filed, but she'd do that later. It didn't matter right now.

"Don't worry about that, your life was in danger. You won't get a ticket for running the red light." He spoke kindly and with a conspiratorial wink that made her want to laugh.

"Thanks, I hope not. Anyway…" She went on to tell him the rest and tried to remember minute details, such as how many there were and all of that, but there wasn't really anything to identify the men by and she had no idea why anyone would want to hurt her.

Other than the fact that she was married to Matteo. She kept that to herself when the cop asked her about enemies. She didn't know who her husband's enemies were, but she knew it must be one of them. They'd tried to kill her to get to Matteo. That terrified her more than she cared to admit, and she looked away from both men. Could she handle this again, if it came down to it? At the moment, she was afraid she couldn't, and that thought made it impossible to look at Matteo. What could she do?

25

atteo's rage was a burning thing that lived deep beneath his heart as he sat with his wife and watched her answer the detective's questions. He saw the moment she realized this was his fault and felt something he thought was shame as an ache deep within his guts. He knew who had done this, and he'd already instructed Anton to deal with it however Anton saw fit.

They both knew what that meant. There was no need to elaborate on the order. Those men had tried to take Marie's life because of a decision he made. They would pay for it.

Matteo watched a doctor come in, inspect Marie's wound, ask her a few questions, and then leave. The man was a good surgeon, one of the best in the state, and he'd put his wife back together. Matteo would make a donation to the hospital's children's ward he decided as he watched a nurse attach another bottle of pain medication to the machine that controlled what went into Marie's IV. Matteo had no idea what they were called, all he cared about was her.

When he'd got the call that his wife had been in an accident and he needed to get to the hospital, he'd driven so fast he knew he'd probably get pulled over or have an accident, but neither happened. He arrived to find Marie had been rushed into surgery and it was hours before she was brought into a room.

Hours that tormented Matteo with their slowness, that gave him time to build up a big fat case of a guilty conscience. Not that he'd caused this, he knew it was likely that the senator's nephew had done this, and if it that was the case, then the senator could kiss his position goodbye and the nephew would find life had suddenly become very short. Very fucking short.

He'd held her hand when they wheeled her into the room and transferred her to her bed. He'd waited, promising her everything under the sun, if she'd just wake up and smile at him. The doctor had explained what had happened to Marie internally and what he'd done to repair it. There was still a risk of bacterial infection because of the nature of the injury.

The surgeon had worked to reassure Matteo that he'd done all he could to ensure the wound was clean and that the laceration was repaired. He'd put her on medicine to stave off an infection and pain medication to help keep her comfortable. That's why she was asleep. It was a very powerful pain medicine.

Anton called in to report what he'd found out so far:

not a whole lot, but he'd seen the car. "Boss, it's a wonder she wasn't killed. The car is riddled with bullets and bullet holes. There must have been at least a hundred gunshots."

"That's not very encouraging," Matteo grunted into the phone.

"No, we need to keep an eye on her, even when she gets out of the hospital. Unless I find those fuckwits that did this first. And whoever put them up to it. I'll be in touch, get back to your wife, boss."

"Thanks, Anton. Take care out there."

Anton had hung up and Matteo went back to his vigil. Now the sun had gone down and the world became much smaller somehow. It was nothing but him and Marie, that was all that existed in this new world. A world where he knew, knew deep down, that he loved this woman.

Trina came in around 7 pm, tears a wet stain on her face. "She was supposed to meet me you know? I had no idea what had happened, why didn't you call me, Matteo? I had to find out from Ma!"

She punched him softly as she came into the room, her stormy eyes even more turbulent as she fell into his arms. "It's alright, Trina, it's not your fault."

"I waited, and waited, and she didn't show. I tried to call but her phone just went to voicemail. I was so scared, Matteo. I tried to call you too, but you didn't answer. Why the fuck didn't you answer?"

"I was... with her, Trina. I just, I was trying to focus on her. And Anton's investigating, so I talked to him, but other than that, I haven't spoken to anyone." He sat down in a hard plastic chair and she joined him on the other one.

"Does she have any family we should call?" From the strain in Trina's voice, Matteo knew she'd been crying for a while and that she was really upset. That touched him because his normally tough as nails little cousin was usually too hard for tears and crying.

"No, not that I know of. It's just us."

"That's so sad, Matteo. She said she wasn't close to her family, but to think that they are that estranged? She's so kind and gentle too. You know she brought me chocolates every time we met? Even when I told her she didn't have to, she would, because she knows I have a sweet tooth. God, I wasn't sure you'd made the right decision when you married this girl, but Matteo, she's something else. Is she alright?" Trina's ramblings finally came to an end and she looked over at him with guarded eyes.

"Yeah, she'll be fine." His reassurance made her smile again. "I'm glad she's touched you in such a way, Trina, because she's one special lady."

"That she is. So, who we killing for this?" Trina's hard gaze told him she wasn't kidding, and he nodded his head. She'd been a part of the family business for a while but had taken a break over the last few months to "get her head straight". She was back in the game then.

"I think it's that Senator I used to have to deal with. Either him or that little upstart family on the other side of the city. I'm not sure."

"There's another possibility you know?" Trina stared at him hard, her gaze a warning.

"No, I don't think Celeste would…" but she interrupted him.

"Oh, come on, we both know the story, Matteo, what happened. This was almost exactly the same. I tell you what, it even makes me wonder about that other family that took the blame. Ever since I heard what happened, I can't stop thinking about it." She sat back in her chair, the tough girl act over for now. Trina was smart, logical, and saw things others wouldn't notice.

"I'll give it some thought," he answered her, but he didn't really want to think about it. It was too close to home and he didn't want to think of his aunt as the kind of person that would kill his wife. Only people that had never met her, that had never known how truly sweet and wonderful she was would want to hurt her.

"See that you do. I know she raised you but that woman is a menace, you've said it yourself before," Trina offered, but Matteo shook his head.

"She's in Italy, how could she…" But he knew how she could arrange this. The Internet had made the world a much smaller place, and anything was possible.

The idea burned a line in his brain that ached so much he put his hand to his head. No, it couldn't be Celeste.

"I think it had something to do with that senator. He came to me not long ago, made some threats to try to let me get his nephew to deal drugs in the Mexican place, you know?" Matteo whispered, in case the cop guarding the door was listening. "I think he got pissed when I cut that shit down from the start. I told him no and why he'd never ask me to do such a thing again, in no uncertain terms. I think this was a threat."

"A what?" Marie asked as she sat up in the bed, her eyes not focusing well for a moment.

"Nothing, baby. You want some water?"

"I'm hungry," she murmured and then smiled when she saw Trina. Marie held her arms out and the other woman came in for a hug. "I'm so glad to see you. I'm sorry I missed out on our spa day. I was trying to get there."

"We'll do it another day, girl, don't you worry," Trina answered, her face buried in Marie's hair as tears started to fall all over again. "I'm just glad you're alright, sweetie."

"I am too. That shit was scary as fuck!" Marie surprised them both with the swear words. Must be the drugs, Matteo thought with a silent chuckle. She'd swear sometimes, but usually only when she was mad or otherwise upset. But then, being gunned down was scary as fuck.

"I'm so proud of you for getting out of that alive." Trina sat back down but she kept a hold on Marie's hand. "I don't know that I could do what you did, girl."

"I panicked, pure and simple," Marie offered, her face tense. "I didn't know what to do, and I froze at first. Then my foot moved, and wouldn't come off the gas pedal, even though I couldn't see. All I could think to do was drive away. I didn't know if they'd follow me, but I didn't care. I was heading for the hospital, trying to get away…"

Matteo took her hand from Trina as her voice trailed off. "You don't have to go through it again."

"But that's just it, Matteo." She turned her face to look at him directly. "I'm dreaming about it, and when I'm awake, it replays over and over in my head. I can't escape it right now. I know I will, maybe tomorrow, maybe next week, but for now, I just see those faces covered in black ski masks as they raised their guns and aimed at me."

"She needs something to help calm her down, have they added that to her medication?" Trina got up, concern making her grumpy.

"Not yet, not with the pain meds she's on. I'll ask the nurse later, if you need me to, alright, Marie?" He'd started off talking to Trina but finished by looking at his wife. She was the one that mattered here.

Suddenly, she was the only thing that mattered to him. He'd known it, deep down, for a very long time, but this today had shaken him. It had shaken him until his love for her had come loose. He wouldn't say anything about it, he didn't see why he should, but he knew it. He felt it.

He loved his wife, which was probably one of the stupidest things a Mafia king could do. It made him vulnerable, open to attack, and it was drilled into him from a young age that he needed to avoid relationships, of any kind.

Celeste had raised him to be cold, dispassionate, ruthless even. All of that had changed in an instant, that long-ago day when he'd first laid eyes on the wonder that was Marie. Now, she was in a hospital bed, a bullet in a plastic bag marked as evidence that the doctor pulled out of her, with stitches in a section of her intestine. He might have given her a life of extravagance and ease, but he'd also brought danger into her life.

Again, that look on her face when she realized that it was Matteo's enemy that had nearly ended her life came back to haunt him. Maybe he should let her go, divorce her, set her up in some nice safe place like Antarctica, where nobody could get to her, and let people forget that she existed. But, to his shame, he knew he couldn't let her go. He'd die without her by his side.

And that was the truth of it. He needed Marie in his life like he needed oxygen. If he pushed her away, divorced her, it would kill him. And if he was any judge of people, she was the same way. She needed him, and if he even mentioned the idea of divorce it would destroy her. She depended on him, loved him, he'd seen it in her eyes more than once. He'd looked away at first, but over time, he'd come to depend on those looks, sometimes merely flashes, come to actually need them to get through his days.

For now, he decided that the best thing to do was to focus on getting her better and letting Anton do his job. He'd take whatever the police said and use that if he could, but he wasn't going to count on them for anything. He knew most of them were good cops, but he also knew plenty of them were on the take, being bribed to look the other way.

He knew that because he'd paid off quite a few in his time. That made them all suspicious, at least in his mind, and even the guard that was posted at Marie's door wasn't above suspicion. He'd stay put until she was released from the hospital, and after that, he'd have his own guards at home and with her when she went out.

"Am I allowed to eat?" Marie asked, her face lit up with hope.

"Not today, baby. Have another sip of water." He handed her the cup and watched her as she took a very careful sip. He'd be there for her. He'd do whatever it took to get her better, and later, when she was safe at home, he'd take care of whoever needed to be taken care of. And he'd bring down the fires of hell on whoever was responsible for this. But only when she was well and safe at home again. Only then.

DARK DESIRES
~ A billionaire dark romance series ~
Dark Desire
Dark Rules
Dark Secret
Dark Time
Dark Truth

BARRE TO BAR
~ A billionaire second chance series ~
Dancing With Lies
Dancing With Temptation
Dancing With Doubt
Dancing With Guilt
Dancing With Redemption

TWISTED INTENTION

~ A billionaire revenge romance series ~
Twisted Beauty
Twisted Love
Twisted Fate

Mafia's Obsession
~ A hot mafia romance series ~
Mafia's Dirty Secret
Mafia's Fake Bride
Mafia's Final Play

Screaming Demons
~ An MC romance series full of suspense ~
Rough Start
Rough Ride
Rough Choice
Rough Patch
Rough Return
Rough Road
Rough Trip
Rough Night
Rough Love

Standalone Contemporary Romance
Billionaire in Vegas
Billionaire Hunt
Billionaire's Game
Billionaire Retreat
Billionaire On Air

A Chance To Love
Somebody To Love
Not Mine To Love

248

Check out Summer's entire collection at
www.summercooper.com/books

ABOUT SUMMER COOPER

Thank you so much for reading. Without you, it wouldn't be possible for me to be a full-time author. I hope you enjoy reading my books as much as I do writing them.

Besides (obviously!) reading and writing, I also love cuddling my dogs, shouting at Alexa, being upside down (aka Yoga) and driving my family cray-cray!

Get in touch at
hello@summercooper.com
www.summercooper.com

facebook.com/summercooperauthor
instagram.com/summercooperauthor
goodreads.com/summercooper
bookbub.com/profile/summer-cooper

www.ingramcontent.com/pod-product-compliance
Lightning Source LLC
Chambersburg PA
CBHW051303210726
48287CB00002B/649